"Luke, did you read Chapter Eight of my book?"

"Look, Princess, the very title of that chapter was enough to turn me off."

"'Courtship Rituals of the American Male'? What's wrong with that? It was supposed to be funny."

Luke pretended to shudder. "I'll admit I fit the American male part, but, Princess, is this a courtship?"

Flushing, Grace snapped, "I realize that running off to a hotel in Cincinnati might mean one thing to a man of your background, but to me—"

"Easy, easy," he soothed. "If we can agree to keep our hands off each other, why can't we drive down to Cincinnati together?"

"For heaven's sake! We are completely different kinds of people."

"Right," Luke agreed. "Think of it as a cultural exchange."

Other books by *Elissa Curry*

Second Chance at Love
TRIAL BY DESIRE #174
WINTER WILDFIRE #178
LADY WITH A PAST #193
BLACK LACE AND PEARLS #213
DATING GAMES #227

To Have and to Hold
PLAYING FOR KEEPS #18
KISS ME, CAIT #23

Elissa Curry *is a former teacher of gifted students, who now employs her own gifts for writing sparkling dialogue and creating inventive plots as a romance author. She lives with her husband and their two young daughters in Indiana, Pennsylvania. The secret of Elissa's compelling romances? "I turn on the music and my word processor, and the stories seem to write themselves."*

Dear Reader:

February is a good month for romance — not only because Valentine's Day falls on the fourteenth, but also because in so much of the country, freezing temperatures and snowy blasts make you want to snuggle up with someone you love. And when you're not curling close, you can read SECOND CHANCE AT LOVE romances! They, too, are guaranteed to keep you toasty warm and wonderfully satisfied.

We begin the month with *Notorious* (#244) by Karen Keast. Many of you wrote in to compliment Karen on the superb job she did on her first book, *Suddenly the Magic* (#255, October 1984). In *Notorious* she's written a boldly sensual variation on *The Taming of the Shrew*, except in this case veterinarian Kate Hollister sets out to domesticate decadent playboy photographer Drew Cambridge — once she realizes she can't resist him, that is! You'll love watching Kate transform this devil-may-care womanizer into a perfect lover . . . and husband!

Have you ever wondered how magicians bend keys and saw people in half? These intriguing secrets — and more! — are revealed in Lee Williams's most original, riveting romance yet — *Under His Spell* (#245). A phony psychic, a sleek, slobbering leopard, and sexy, black-garbed magician Julian Sharpe make *Under His Spell* an unforgettable romance with a *very* magic touch.

We were pleased and impressed with Carole Buck's first romance for us, *Encore* (#219, September 1984). Now *Intruder's Kiss* (#246) establishes her as one of our brightest talents. I love the opening: Sara Edwards, armed with a squash racquet, is about to tackle two noisy intruders — who turn out to be a huge sheep dog and charming, devastating Matt Michaels. Although wildly attracted to Matt (not the dog!), Sara begins to wonder: Just who *is* Matt Michaels? You'll be delightfully entertained by this lively, sexy, fun-filled tale.

Few writers capture the sizzling chemistry between a hero and heroine better than Elissa Curry. In *Lady Be Good*

(#247), she creates two truly unique characters: Etiquette columnist Grace Barrett is poised and polished, perfectly coiffed and regally mannered; Luke "the Laser" Lazurnovich is an ex-football player who pretends to be even more uncouth than he really is. To tell how this ill-matched pair comes to realize they're perfect for each other, Elissa combines a delicious sense of humor with the endearing tenderness of an emotionally involving love story.

In her outstanding debut, *Sparring Partners* (#177, February 1984), Lauren Fox immediately established herself as a master of witty dialogue. Now, very much in the Lauren Fox tradition, comes *A Clash of Wills* (#248), which pits calm, controlled stockbroker Carrie Carstairs against outrageous, impulsive, infuriatingly stubborn investor/inventor Harlen Matthews. As you can imagine, they're an explosive combination. *A Clash of Wills* is wonderfully fresh and inventive.

You'll be *Swept Away* by our last February SECOND CHANCE AT LOVE romance, #249 by Jacqueline Topaz. "Cleaning woman" Paula Ward has dusted Tom Clinton's penthouse and is "borrowing" his lavish bathroom to prepare for a date, when the devastating millionaire arrives home — with guests! To save her job, Paula impulsively agrees to pose as Tom's wife — with funny, sad, and, above all, sensuous results . . .

February's SECOND CHANCE AT LOVE romances are sure to chase away your winter blahs. So enjoy them — and keep warm!

With best wishes,

Ellen Edwards

Ellen Edwards, Senior Editor
SECOND CHANCE AT LOVE
The Berkley Publishing Group
200 Madison Avenue
New York, N.Y. 10016

Second Chance at Love®

LADY
BE GOOD

ELISSA CURRY

SECOND CHANCE AT LOVE
BOOK

LADY BE GOOD

First edition published February 1985

First printing

"Second Chance at Love" and the butterfly emblem are trademarks belonging to Jove Publications, Inc.

Printed in the United States of America

Second Chance at Love books are published by
The Berkley Publishing Group
200 Madison Avenue, New York, NY 10016

With thanks to my husband, who was not the inspiration for this book, thank heavens, but who did supply much of the "color."

CHAPTER ONE

Dear Ms. Barrett,
  *I never thought I'd find myself writing to an eti-
quette columnist for advice, but here I am. My problem is complicated...*

Aren't they all, thought Grace Barrett as she sat in the
lobby of the Pittsburgh Hilton, reading the last letter in the
packet forwarded from her syndicate in New York.

  *My daughter is getting married next month to a
perfectly awful young man with whom she's been cohabitating for the last three years, and they've decided
to have a big wingding of a wedding—much to my
recently retired husband's financial dismay. Not only
are we balking at paying such a huge sum for a wedding, but my daughter insists on having the occasion
in Cleveland, and we live in Albany, New York. My
husband claims to have a terrible fear of airplanes,
and threatens to get horribly drunk before making the
trip and stay that way throughout the weekend. I sus-*

1

pect his threat has more to do with our prospective son-in-law than airplanes. What should we do? Stay at home and send a check to cover our expenses?
—*Agitated in Albany*

Of course not, Grace decided flippantly, and she wrote neatly on her pad:

Dear Agi:
Take the train. It's so much more civilized. Arriving at an airport while under the influence of alcohol is rather gauche, but to do so in a train station is sometimes considered charming or romantic, as if you've been sipping champagne in a private car while watching the scenery pass by. Perhaps your husband's behavior will be interpreted as delirious happiness. On the other hand, if you don't go to the wedding, your friends and family will know exactly why. Bite the bullet and go to the wedding even if it is in Cleveland.

Unfortunately, Grace thought as she clicked her gold Cross pen closed and slid it neatly into the side pocket of her traveling attaché, trains don't always run to Cleveland. Not from Pittsburgh at five-thirty in the afternoon, that is, and not in the midst of snowstorms. Not even so that stranded syndicated columnists suffering book promotion tours could get to their next television interviews scheduled less than twenty-four hours away. Grace was stuck in Pittsburgh.

The lobby of the Hilton was already a madhouse, with frantic guests either checking out in hopes of beating the storm or despondently checking in for the duration of the predicted snowfall. If that blasted limousine didn't hurry, Grace was going to be stranded, too, and miss her engagement in Cleveland, and then the publicity department at the publishing house was going to be furious. Well, not furious, perhaps, for Lucy Simons was really a very coolheaded woman under the worst conditions. But rescheduling these television appearances and coordinating the local release of books was like asking Hannibal to please hold the elephants halfway up the Alps another few days, and Grace wanted to avoid straining Lucy's good humor. The book promotion tour was only three days along, and with two weeks to go, Grace realized she was off to a shaky start. She didn't want to miss getting to Cleveland!

"Miss Barrett?" The assistant hotel manager approached with the sideways scuttle of an anxious crab. He was a perspiring young man who had been assigned to keeping the notoriously formidable Ms. Grace Barrett comfortable for the last day and a half, and although Grace was convinced that she didn't *really* pay attention to how people behaved, this poor fellow tried very hard to mind his p's and q's. He tried *too* hard.

He was looking relieved, Grace saw, so she immediately rose from the chair in which she'd been seated, catching up on her work. As always, she was calm and poised and gracious. "You're about to get rid of me, Mr. Sansone?"

The young man smiled nervously and reached for her luggage. "Yes, ma'am. I mean, we're sorry to see you go, of course, but—"

"Yes, yes," Grace said smoothly. She took up her attaché case and coat and imperiously allowed him to heft both her suitcases. "The car has arrived for me?"

"Yes, ma'am. This way. We're terribly sorry for the delay. If you'll allow me . . ."

He shoved through the revolving door, and Grace followed, her mink-collared black cashmere coat over her arm and the matching cap tucked safely into the sleeve. For the short walk from the hotel to the covered drive, her wool suit and suede boots would provide plenty of protection from the whipping wind. Her blond hair, usually swept primly back from her heart-shaped face with its Bostonian nose and Great-grandmother Lendwell's flawless mouth, was instantly blown into a cyclone around her head by the blast of winter wind. Grace did not lose her poise, however. A bit of a breeze was invigorating. Mother said so often.

Through the wind-whipped snow, the driver came striding around the hood of the black limousine, stuffing his big hands into a pair of tattered gloves with the sheepskin lining showing through the splits in the seams. His hands were the first thing Grace saw, for he reached for the handle of the back door just as she arrived at the curbside.

"Hello," he said.

"Ms. Barrett is in quite a hurry," said the assistant manager swiftly. "You're hours late already! If you think for one minute—"

"There's a storm going on," the driver interrupted laconically, turning to the manager, "in case you didn't notice, pal."

The driver was huge. Six feet three or more, Grace guessed, with the build of a longshoreman. He had a gigantic blue parka on, huge boots with waffled soles, and a black and gold knit cap pulled tightly down around his ears against the cold. Towering over the inadequately dressed Mr. Sansone, he exuded not only the threat of sheer size, but also an embarrassing amount of common sense.

Grace intervened smoothly as she prepared to climb into the long, low car. "Let's not argue about the obvious, shall we? Good afternoon, Mr. Sansone. Thank you for your assistance during my stay."

"Of course, Ms. Barrett," said the assistant manager as he hastily got out of the way and allowed the driver to slam the car door behind her. Grace's last glimpse of the officious Sansone was obliterated by a fresh blast of snow. She settled into the seat, laid her coat carefully beside her, and reached to smooth her straight blond hair.

In another instant, the driver got in and whammed his own door shut. He tugged his cap off and shook his head hard to get rid of the clinging flakes of snow. He blew a noisy "Whew!" and declared, "Some night!"

Grace allowed herself an affirmatively murmured "Quite."

He turned to face her, one long arm thrown across the back of the seat between them. "Now, then. You're not really headed for the airport, are you, lady?"

He was not just big, but older than Grace had first guessed. Perhaps in his mid thirties. He wasn't a young kid working his way through college, that was certain. His curly brown hair was too long and a little wild, but shot through with an honest streak of gray just to the left of a widow's peak. He was blue-eyed, a fact that was unremarkable except for the clarity of that blueness, and impossibly thick, girlish lashes surrounded those lazy-lidded eyes. The rest of his face could politely be called rugged. It was narrow, with sharply cut planes and the fresh burn of wind and winter sunshine on his skin. He'd broken a cheekbone once, Grace supposed, judging by the asymmetry of his face, and his front teeth were either absolutely perfect or expensively capped. She guessed the latter. He looked like the type who might have lost a few teeth in a fistfight. His grin slipped downward on one side of his face, and he had a slight cleft in his chin although it was obscured by the stubble of at least two days' growth of beard. His mouth was crooked, but somehow sensually so, and his nose must also have been broken before, for its aquiline line wasn't quite straight. A tough-looking customer except for his delightfully natural smile.

He must have seen her startled reaction, for he laughed at her. "Whatsamatter? I thought all New York ladies were used to obnoxious cabdrivers."

There were many responses, of course. Grace was in the business of quick retorts. It had often been her job to advise people on the most effective way to establish a cool though non-hostile relationship with household help, employees, and the like. The storm, the lateness of the hour, the tension of the day, and the upcoming white-knuckle flight to Cleveland were all factors in shaking Grace's usually unshakable demeanor, however. Startled, she asked, "Why do you imagine that I'm from New York?"

His grin didn't waver, and his blue gaze slid meaningfully down the sleek lines of her wool suit. "It's written all over you, lady. Except you talk like you were raised in Boston, sent to finishing school in England, and went to Katie Gibbs for the standard course. Am I right?"

Further jolted, Grace asked in astonishment, "What do you know about Katharine Gibbs?"

He threw back his head and laughed again, then spun

around in his seat and reached for the ignition. "Whatdya think? We're too provincial out here in Steeltown?"

"I never meant to imply that—"

"I know, I know. Airport, right?"

In exasperation, Grace gave up. "Right."

He gunned the engine and whipped the wheel over, sending the big car around the circular drive and into the street. The back tires slid in the slush going out and bumped the curb, throwing Grace against the door. She grabbed for support and hung on.

"Sorry," he said happily, without glancing into the rearview mirror at her. "I'm not used to this monster. We don't get many calls for the limo unless it's time for the senior proms."

"I see," Grace murmured, summoning her poise.

"So you must be somebody special to have the Hilton hiring a private car when they've got their own buses. You with U.S. Steel? Or a government type?"

"Neither," Grace answered, sedate once more. "I'm a writer."

"Oh, yeah?" His blue eyes immediately flashed in the rearview mirror. "You mean books?"

"Book," Grace corrected. "One."

"I get it," he said, nodding. He tugged at the zipper of his parka, getting comfortable as he steered the car around the next corner. "You're going around the country, talking about your book on TV, right?"

"As a matter of fact, yes."

"How's it going so far? You like traveling?"

"Until today, everything has been rather smooth."

"Umm," he said sympathetically. "The winters around here can kill you. Where are you headed now? If you're going to the airport, I mean."

There had to be a graceful way of terminating such a familiar conversation, but none was coming to mind. Grace found herself oddly interested in the back of the driver's head, with its gently curling dark hair that was . . . well, *fleecy* was the word that seemed to describe it best. His face was rough, his body big and thuglike, but his hair looked soft and rather nice curling around the nape of his neck and tickling his ears. The collar of a flannel shirt in a red Stewart tartan showed through the loosened top of his parka. He had a navy turtleneck cotton sweater under that, too. His shoulders were undoubtedly immense, although it was hard to tell under so many layers of warm clothing.

Heavens! Grace thought. She was ogling a man! That certainly showed what state of mind had befallen her! She forced herself to remember the man's question and said primly, "Cleveland, as a matter of fact."

"Cleveland!" he objected with a hoot of laughter. "Lady, you're never gonna get there! Not tonight!"

"Yes, I will," Grace said firmly, turning her head so that she glared out at the foul weather. "Don't tell me otherwise, please. It's taking all the courage I have to get on this airplane tonight, so don't talk me out of it."

"What?" he asked, curious immediately. He glanced up briefly into the mirror, then down again to negotiate the car onto a bridge.

"I'm not making any sense," Grace agreed, and she smoothed her hair back into place more carefully. She was confiding in a perfect stranger, for some reason, and it renewed her feeling of discomfort. It had to be the unfortunate circumstances in which she found herself, she decided, and turned her face to the snowy window to hide her expression. "I have a fear of flying," she said to the window. "I've been taking trains until now, but there seems to be no way to get from Pittsburgh to Cleveland tonight except by air."

"You picked a great night to overcome your phobia," he noted with a grin in the mirror.

"Perhaps I'll have a cocktail before takeoff," Grace said, thinking of the letter she'd just answered.

"Make it a double and maybe you won't see Cleveland. Trust me, you don't *want* to see Cleveland, not even buried in three feet of snow. Of course, you can't expect a Pittsburgher ever to say anything nice about Cleveland." He glanced into the side mirror, used the back of his glove to rub some of the fog off the car window, then accelerated into traffic. The car nosed into another lane and headed for a tunnel. With traffic safely negotiated, he asked, "So what's it about? Your book, I mean. A romantic novel or a tome on foreign policy?"

The question stumped Grace. Not the question, precisely, but how to answer it. To a prince or a gentleman who owned his own evening clothes, she could say the title and be done with it. But *Ms. Barrett's Etiquette for Every Occasion* was going to baffle this character completely. Or cause him to laugh uproariously. To play it safe, she said, "It's a revised version of a nonfiction book my mother wrote several years ago."

"Oh, yeah? Who's your mother? Anyone I'd have heard of?"

"Perhaps," Grace said, giving in cautiously. "My mother is Dear Mrs. Barrett."

"Dear—? Hey, no kidding?" he demanded in delight, seeking her reflection in the mirror again. "You mean the good-manners lady? The one who writes for the newspapers? Like Dear Abby?"

"Dear Abby," Grace corrected swiftly, "deals with a totally different subject. Ours is exclusively an etiquette column."

"'Ours'? Hey, do you write for the newspaper, too? You must. You said you were a writer."

"My mother has retired," Grace said with hauteur. "Until this year I've been her assistant—"

"—but now you're taking charge. Nice going!" He complimented her with another wide smile. "You've published a new version of the same old book to launch your career. Good thinking."

He was surprisingly smart for a limousine driver, Grace decided. And even though he looked fairly scruffy, he used an occasional three-syllable word and conveyed a worldliness she found intriguing. She was rarely intrigued by men these days, and never by men who drove her cars or carried her luggage or ran the elevator in her East Side apartment building. This one was different. Or maybe she was just looking for a way to keep her mind off the airplane ride she was soon going to endure.

"So how are sales? Is your book a big success?"

"That's difficult to say," Grace told him. "It's just been released, you understand."

"Sure." He nodded knowledgeably. "But your tour is bound to boost sales. How many cities are you doing?"

"Ten. Two down, eight to go."

"Philly, Pittsburgh, Cleveland," he guessed. "Then what? Chicago? Detroit?"

"First Cincinnati. Then Detroit, St. Louis, Kansas City, Chicago, and finally Dallas."

"Oh, yeah? Even St. Louis? That's my hometown. Nothing out West?"

"Not yet. Perhaps in another month. My mother suggested I try traveling a bit at a time, not all at once." It was crazy to ask him anything in return, but Grace felt she should stop talking about herself. Hoping to get a long, wordy response that she could politely tune out, she inquired, "What brought you to Pittsburgh if you're from St. Louis?"

He smiled at her in the mirror. "Got something against Pittsburgh?"

"Of course not," she said quickly. "I simply—"

"I know, I know. Easy, there. I ended up here after college, that's all. Now I'm in business."

"In business?" Grace repeated in spite of herself.

Clearly, he'd heard her skeptical tone of voice. "Sure," he said defensively. "Oh, I get it. No, I don't drive these things very often—honest. Can't you tell?" He pulled the car out of the tunnel and into the driving snow once more, explaining cheerfully, "I run a garage, that's all. We keep a couple of these limos around to make a few bucks, and the Hilton owes me some favors. They call when they need to run somebody special out to the airport. All my employees went home for the day. I live out this way, so it makes things easy."

Grace assimilated all that information carefully. College, business, "running" a garage. Did that mean owning it? And why would the Hilton owe this scruffy character any favors?

"I'll make it easy for you," he said suddenly, with another grin in the mirror. He had apparently guessed the direction of her thoughts. "Around this town, I'm a minor celebrity, too. I used to play football."

"Football?" Grace repeated stupidly.

"Yeah. You know. The Pittsburgh Steelers. Ever heard of them?"

"Oh, of course!" He was a professional football player! That made perfect sense, Grace thought. No wonder he was the size of the Abominable Snowman. "Yes, now I see!"

He laughed again at her startled tone of voice. "Did you think I made my living breaking kneecaps for the Mob?"

"N-no, certainly not, but—" Good grief, Grace Barrett was stuttering!

"I'm only kidding," he assured her. "About the Mob, I mean. My name's Luke Lazurnovich."

Of course. In a town like Pittsburgh, he would have a romantic name with lots of syllables. Grace said mildly, "How do you do?"

Mocking her round vowels, he teased her by repeating, "Howww do you dooo? You're Ms. Barrett. What's your first name? Elizabeth? Victoria? Anastasia? It's got to be something snooty."

With a snap, she supplied, "Grace."

He laughed again. "No kidding? Princess Grace! You look like her. Grace Kelly, I mean. I love it!"

Well, one learns lessons like this all the time, of course, Grace thought. If one encourages perfect strangers in conversation, they soon take liberties and become overly familiar. She had brought it on herself by breaking one of her own hard-and-fast rules: Never treat anyone with friendship unless you intend to continue the relationship.

Well, she was already too deeply into these socially dangerous waters. The best way to avoid talking about herself was to talk about him. Quickly, she took an inventory of her supply of football trivia and inquired, "What position did you play, Mr. Lazur—Lazurnovich?"

"Call me Luke. Nobody uses Lazurnovich, not even my

own mother. For the Steelers? I played wide receiver." Then he asked, "Know anything about football?"

Grace smiled, but tried to cover it with her fingertips. He wasn't going to let her get away with anything, and rightly so. She shook her head and admitted, "Only that the Rose Bowl is an excuse for a wonderful parade."

He grinned once again. "Not as good as Macy's Thanksgiving parade. I love those big balloons. Underdog, remember him?"

"Yes, of course." Grace felt herself warming to Luke Lazurnovich, for any big lug who sided with Underdog, the caped canine cartoon character, couldn't be all bad. Aloud, she said, "I thought professional football players always worked on holidays."

"I wasn't born a football player, of course. And I've been out of the game for three years." Suddenly, he added an exclamation. "Yipes!"

The car lurched, lost its grip on the road, and slid sideways just enough to send an instant shot of adrenaline through Grace's system. The weather was getting worse, and it was officially dark by now. The snow looked like flashes of white light as the wind drove it against the windshield. Luke Lazurnovich had slowed the big car to a sedate speed, but the road was still hazardous.

"Are we going to make it?" she asked, sitting forward on the seat to look apprehensively at the blowing snow.

"To the airport? Sure. You're not going to get to Cleveland, though. If the weather's lousy here, it's worse up there. I'll bet their airport's closed by now."

"Don't say that," Grace said prayerfully. "I've got to be there by mid-afternoon tomorrow."

"Heck, you've got plenty of time, then. It's only a couple hours' drive from here."

"Driving looks less likely than flying," Grace observed.

"You've got a point there," he said.

The highway was completely obscured by snow or blown clear in other patches by the increasing wind. There were already cars parked along the shoulder, as if their drivers had prudently given up the attempt to negotiate the dangerous road. The limousine, however, was a heavier car and managed to plow through the drifts without mishap. Luke Lazurnovich was a good driver to boot, and he took his time and concentrated. Fortunately, he wasn't the kind of man to show his anxiety, if he was feeling any.

"There," he said after a few more minutes. "You can see the lights from the airport now. At least everybody hasn't gone home to bed yet."

He was right. The airport looked busy and friendly, and Grace subsided into the back seat once more, enjoying the last few moments before she had to brave the cold winter air. She gathered up her attaché case and found her good calfskin gloves inside. She pulled them onto her slim hands as Luke Lazurnovich drove the limousine around the curve at the entrance. He parked illegally at the end of the covered walkway, shut off the engine, and got out.

Grace waited until he had retrieved her luggage and then came around to open the door for her.

"What airline?" he asked as he helped her out onto the sidewalk.

He had pulled her easily out of the car, and Grace took a step to catch her balance. The man was strong! On a breath, she said, "USAIR."

He nodded, shouldering the strap of her carryall effortlessly. "This way, then."

Grace had to trot to catch him, her high-heel boots clattering on the icy pavement. "Look, I can hire someone to help me with those. You needn't—"

"Inside," he ordered calmly. "I'm freezing out here."

Grace accompanied him into the terminal, still objecting. "I'm quite capable of handling my own travel arrangements now, Mr. Lazur—"

"Luke. It's no trouble. If Cleveland is closed, though, you're going to get stuck here, and that would be miserable. Come on. We'll just check the board and see if your flight's been canceled."

"It will not be canceled!" Grace insisted with growing annoyance as she hurried to keep up with his long strides.

He was a very big man, and he didn't seem to notice that her sleek skirt, for all its style and elegance, prevented her from matching his steps.

He halted in front of a bank of television screens and scanned them rapidly. For Grace, a woman who hadn't flown on an airplane since she was fourteen, the technology looked unfamiliar and rather disconcerting. It wasn't like a train station. This place was blazingly bright. At the nearby ticket counters there were lines of baggage-laden people looking either frantic or woebegone. Vivid travel posters screamed from the walls, and a garish collection of multi-colored flags swung from the high ceiling. The place looked like a science-fiction circus, and the noise was incredible.

"You're in luck," Luke said, pointing at a television with his free hand. "Is it flight 314? It's still on the board. Do you want that drink? You've got half an hour."

Grace swallowed involuntarily, staring at the blinking letters on the television screen. Up until now, she'd been bluffing herself. Or perhaps hoping that Luke Lazurnovich was right and that the plane was not going to take off. She hated to fly, and over the years her distaste for it had mush-roomed into a definite fear. Now that she was confronted with the reality of stepping onto one of those death traps, she was worried. No, not worried. Scared.

"There's a bar up this way," said Luke, translating her silence easily. "It can't hurt to have a drink. Maybe some-thing to eat, too? A sandwich?"

"I don't dare," said Grace as she willingly followed him away from the televisions. "I'll embarrass myself later."

He laughed. "And you're supposed to have perfect man-ners! How does one upchuck in a socially acceptable way on an airplane, Princess Grace?"

"Let's hope I don't have to find out," she retorted, giving him a wry smile.

He met the look directly, with a twinkle of understanding in his blue gaze. He was attractive, Grace realized with a jolt. He had the battered look of a movie tough guy, but his smile and his unflinching gaze bespoke a gentler man inside. And he wasn't a boor. Not exactly, she qualified. He didn't have the polish of Fred Astaire, but he wasn't making even a subtle protest about carrying her luggage, which Grace knew was very heavy indeed. A lesser man would have left her on the curb outside and gone home to his warm house. And probably to his wife and kids.

Dear Ms. Barrett,
   What is the proper etiquette for flirting with a married man?

   —Pensive in Pittsburgh

Dear Pen,
   Ms. Barrett gives you two choices: Don't, and don't.

Suddenly Grace had an uncanny urge to know whether Luke Lazurnovich and a wife and children.

His grin widened and he jerked his head to indicate one of the concourses. "This way. We'll find you a drink."

In the next few moments, as they strolled up through the crowded terminal together, Grace learned something very interesting about professional football players. Because of their size, they drew the eye of every passerby, both male and female. The men looked hard and narrow-eyed at Luke, as if trying to decide if he was someone they ought to remember, and the women looked him up and down and finished by smiling directly into his face. *All* the women did it— from teenage gigglers to grandmotherly types!

One young woman dressed in a pair of jeans so tight that they might have been surgically attached to her skin gave him such an eyelash flutter that Grace wondered if the poor woman had a cinder in her eye. The sexual message was obvious. *Anytime, Big Boy.* Blue Jeans appraised Luke's sloppy jacket and the snug way his worn corduroy trousers clung to his lean hips. Grace could see the other woman's gaze travel lasciviously across the flanneled expanse of Luke's chest. Even the most annoying construction workers in Manhattan used more finesse than that!

Luke seemed blithely unaware of the attention he drew. He had a smile for everyone who caught his eye, though, and that certainly didn't discourage anyone.

He found the bar and pushed the glass door open for Grace to enter first. She slipped past his tall frame, a task in itself because of his size and her own above-average height, and she brushed his chest with her shoulder. The contact surprised her. She didn't usually pay attention to such casual contact, but this packed a punch, it seemed. No, no, the flash of static had to exist only in her unguarded imagination. Impossible that there should be another explanation. For Grace, this was the equivalent of Princess Di being sexually attracted to Stanley Kowalski of *A Streetcar Named Desire* fame. She must have imagined it.

Thoughtfully, she entered the cool dimness of the cocktail lounge. A new breed of animal, this Luke Lazurnovich. New to her, at least. She'd never been around a man so physically charismatic who was so comfortable with his celebrity status and the sexual come-ons that went with it.

He plunked her suitcase down on the floor. There wasn't an available seat in the room, for apparently other travelers had come to the bar to bolster their courage. Luke turned to her. "Well? What'll it be? What does a well-bred lady order in a bar?"

"A gimlet, please," Grace requested without a blink.

He blinked, however. "No kidding? Not a whiskey sour or something with a little umbrella and a bunch of fruit?"

"Just a twist, thank you," Grace said, and she spotted a pair of businessmen leaving their seats at the bar. She gave them half a second to vacate and then she headed for the empty chairs like a starved barracuda.

Luke flagged the bartender. "One gimlet with a twist and a draft, huh?"

The bartender waved his towel once in acknowledgment, and Luke followed Grace to the seats she had staked out. People got out of his way, giving Luke plenty of room. They looked up at him as he passed. He didn't seem aware of it and arrived beside Grace. "Not exactly the Plaza, right?"

"Every establishment has a flavor of its own," she responded tactfully, folding her coat in her lap.

"Come on," he pressed, his blue eyes wickedly sparkling under their sleepy-looking lids. He spread open his parka and sat beside her, turning the chair outward so his long legs could stretch in comfort. He didn't appear to care that his scruffy trousers were marked with a perfect handprint of automotive grease. "You're a classy lady. This place isn't your cup of tea."

"I'm not a frequent patron of places like this," Grace admitted coolly as she removed her gloves and laid them on the bar. "But I don't condemn them. To each his own. Within reason, that is."

He laughed. He put his elbow on the bar and relaxed. "Yeah? That's an interesting outlook from a lady who writes about etiquette, I think."

"We needn't discuss my work," she responded, firmly turning the conversation away from etiquette. All she needed was to get into an argument about gracious living with a pro football player. "I instruct people on the correct ways to handle social situations, but I try not to judge their behavior."

"Okay," he said easily, having understood perfectly the message she was really communicating. "I hate talking about football, too, to tell you the truth," he remarked. "We can talk about anything else, can't we?"

She hadn't intended to end up sitting here with this man. How had it happened? Grace asked herself. Usually she was so careful. Except for her ex-fiancé, Kip, Grace hadn't spent any time in the last eight years one-on-one with any man. And this was much more man than Grace could comfortably cope with. He was gigantic. But not scary. Not yet, anyway. She smiled ruefully then and teased him with the stereotypical opener, "Beastly weather we've been having, don't you think?"

He laughed and played along, asking, "What's your sign? No, no, forget I mentioned that! You've probably never set foot in a singles' bar in your life. How old are you, anyway?"

"That, you should know, is a question that a gentleman never asks a lady."

"I've never been accused of being a gentleman," he cracked, "so we're safe. I'm interested, that's all. You act like you're somebody's grandmother, but you look about twenty-five in spite of that Coco Chanel style of dressing you've adopted. How old? Thirty?"

Since their drinks did not arrive at that moment to save her from having an answer, Grace gave up and said, "Thirty-one."

He whistled appreciatively and smiled. "Just right."

"For what, may I ask?"

"Ah, the drinks. Your gimlet, I believe?"

The bartender set the small glass on a paper napkin in front of Grace, and a frothy mug of beer at Luke's elbow. Before Grace could reach for her attaché case, Luke pulled some folded bills from his pocket and pushed a five across at the bartender.

The man took the money but eyed Luke a moment longer. At the silence, Luke lifted his head and the bartender snapped his fingers. "Luke the Laser!"

Luke smiled broadly and countered jokingly, "You sure about that?"

The bartender grinned. "You are, aren't you? Luke 'the Laser' Lazurnovich! I won fifty bucks because of that pass you caught against Oakland five years ago! Remember that one?"

"Sure," Luke said agreeably. "I'm glad you won something."

":Man!" the bartender exclaimed with pleasure. "It's really you! Hey, the drinks are on the house. For your lady friend, too."

"Thanks," Luke said, and he turned his shoulder slightly to indicate that his conversation with the bartender was over. It was a classic gesture, one without the element of total rejection. Grace hadn't seen it done so subtly in many years. It was an art to tell people to get lost without hurting their feelings. Most people were smart enough to understand the slight turning of the shoulder if it was executed as precisely as Luke had just done it. The bartender got the message but gave Luke's shoulder a comradely pat before he left.

Grace found that Luke's eyes were fastened on hers. She smiled and nodded after the bartender. "That was smoothly done, Laser."

He shrugged humbly and reached for his beer. "It's all in knowing how. To your health, Princess."

Grace sipped her drink and at first didn't taste the liquor. She was too busy soaking up impressions of Luke Lazurnovich. This wasn't Grace's, milieu, of course. She usually traveled in social circles where men and women were properly introduced and then spent many hours in the company of others in sedate sitting rooms before daring to see each other alone. Luke Lazurnovich possessed an easy manner, one that seemed harmless enough, in fact. He didn't have the hard-sell patter that Grace had unconsciously expected of a man from his background. He was casual and friendly, and he didn't hint about sex or look her over as if he were trying to guess her weight or the numbers printed on her brassiere. His manner was comforting, she decided. She was safe in his company.

Luke drained a good three inches of his beer before setting the mug down on the bar. He touched the back of his hand to his mouth, then looked Grace straight in the eye. "Well," he said cheerfully, "if your plane gets canceled, you want to come back to my place for the night?"

CHAPTER TWO

Dear Ms. Barrett,
How does a lady politely say no to a gentleman
and make it stick?

—Weak-Willed in Wisconsin

Dear Weak,
Your two choices are simple: one, firmly but with
a smile; and two, weakly, but with a smile—then give
in.

"It's very kind of you to offer," Grace said calmly, once
she had wiped the startled look off her face, "but I'm sure
the plane will go off as scheduled."

"Is that good or bad?" he asked, undaunted. "I mean, if
you're nervous about flying, it might be better to spend the
night with me instead."

"Your logic is perfect," Grace commented wryly. "But
before I get myself entangled in something I'm certainly
going to regret later, I—"

"It's not like I'm asking you to settle down and raise a family, y'know," he said earnestly, his dark brows lifting over his baby-blue eyes. "You're going to have a problem in about ten minutes—seven if you're a fast drinker. The plane is going to be canceled and you're going to be stuck, and I guarantee there won't be an available hotel room in ten miles even if the weather lets up enough so people can get that far away."

"Are you familiar with the concept of crossing bridges when one comes to them?" Grace inquired sweetly.

With a grin, he shrugged, giving up. Then he reached for his beer again. "How about saving for a rainy day? Or the early bird catching the worm? Or the ever-popular boy scout motto?"

"'Be prepared'? Are we talking about you or me?"

He laughed. "You're neat. Classy, but not as snooty as I first thought."

"Thank you," Grace responded primly. She decided that Luke wasn't as bad as she'd first thought, either. In spite of his rough clothes and touseled hair, he had an intelligent face and a quick mind. Match truth with truth, she thought, and see what happens. Fortified by another sip of her drink, she added with a twinkle in her eyes, "And you aren't as much of a clod as I expected."

"Oh, I'm a clod all right," he corrected with a grin that shone over the rim of his mug. "But I'm happy that way. Ignorance is bliss. Pigs are happiest when they're—no, no. Is this really acceptable small talk, Dear Ms. Barrett, or have we digressed into outright insults?"

"I try not to insult, honestly," Grace explained, after another swallow that gave her a half-second to think. She knew she'd gotten off to a bad start with this man, and she was curiously anxious to set him straight. Making an unusual effort to clarify her position on good manners and the human condition, she said, "If I've insulted you, I apologize. After all, there is so much unpleasantness in the world already. Why should knowledgeable people add to it by acting like barbarians?"

"It makes life more interesting?" Luke suggested.

"Sparkling conversation is much more entertaining."

"But harder to come by unless you live with Dick Cavett and invite William F. Buckley, Jr., for brunch on Sunday."

Grace laughed. "Even Bill Buckley enjoys delivering a good insult, I'm afraid."

"So you fight rudeness by being superpolite to insensitive dolts like me?"

"It doesn't always work, but I feel as if *I* haven't stooped to behaving like an insensitive dolt. Which you are not, I don't think."

"But already you're starting to talk like me," he pointed out with relish, smiling mischievously. "With my sentences backward. I'm a bad influence. Wait and see, it'll get worse. What d'you think? You want to come back to my place?"

"Good grief!" Grace exclaimed, her eyes widening as she stared at him with a mixture of amused delight and growing respect. "How did a football player come to think the way you do?" she teased.

"Fast, you mean?" he asked, enjoying her expression with a delighted grin of his own. "Is there supposed to be a ten-second lapse while an idea makes its way along my damaged nerve endings? Wide receivers get hit in the head, but not that often."

Laughing genuinely, Grace shook her head and reached for her drink. Aloud, she said to herself, "I'm beginning to see why Lucy suggested I needed a promotion tour."

"Lucy? A friend of yours?"

"My closest," Grace agreed without hesitating to make this personal disclosure. The warmth created by her gimlet was working its magic already, thawing the tension that had been building inside her for hours. This wasn't bad, sitting in the semidarkness with a man who looked a bit like Conan the Barbarian but had a surprisingly quick wit. No this wasn't bad at all. Grace said willingly, "Lucy's also the publicist for my book. She says I need to get out of New York and look around."

"Lucy sounds like a smart lady."

"One of the smartest."

"What do you suppose she wanted you to look at outside

Manhattan?" he asked, wrapping one of his big hands around the glass mug and then lifting it to take another long pull from his beer.

Grace gave in to the casual atmosphere of her surroundings and crossed one long slender leg over the other, making sure that her skirt clung modestly around her knees. She explained, "Lucy has an ongoing romance with New York, but she thinks other people ought to enjoy the wonders of rural America and return to tell her about things."

"Like the men of Middle America?"

"Exactly," Grace agreed, eyeing Luke Lazurnovich's long, relaxed, and superbly masculine body with a sidelong glance. He really was an astonishing specimen of the male animal. He didn't have the well-tended, carefully dieted look of the Nautilus pseudo-jock, for his body was flexible and loose-limbed. His was a graceful pose, not an artful, practiced posture calculated to show off his pectorals or laboriously honed bicepses. New York seemed full of those men these days, and the Caribbean beaches were even worse. Prettily conditioned bodies whose muscles were not used for work but simply to adorn seemed unnecessary and therefore ridiculous to Grace. Luke was different. Half his awesomeness was that he knew precisely how to use his body without having to think about it. Grace released an unconsciously pent-up breath and added with significant wryness, "Lucy would love you, that's certain."

"I affect a lot of women that way, for some reason," he countered lightly, having watched as she studied first his chest and solid abdomen, then his snug corduroys and his lean yet muscular thighs. He began to smile anew. "It's a burden I've learned to cope with somehow."

Grace laughed at his self-mocking humility. "Lucy is clever enough to see past a man's outward appearance. It's just that she doesn't choose to do it often enough."

"I like her already," Luke said, watching with a glimmer of light in his eyes while Grace sipped from her glass. Abruptly, he asked, "Does she pick up men in airport bars and offer to show them the sights of New York?"

Grace choked on her drink. Luke reached and patted her

kindly between her shoulder blades. Surely he wasn't under the assumption that she was picking him up? No, she could see he was only joking. "Laser, you're definitely too fast for me. This isn't my style at all."

"You really did need to get out of New York," he said decisively, sitting back in his chair once more. "Because I'm an amateur when it comes to this flirtatious banter."

"Is that what this is?" Grace asked, still with her hand pressed delicately to her throat. "Flirtatious banter? Have you a pencil? I think I should be taking notes for the next edition of my book."

"*Ms. Barrett Goes to the Disco*?" he suggested.

Grace laughed again. "My mother would have a stroke!"

He tipped his head curiously and his eyes were suddenly sharp. "Does Mother's health depend on her daughter's behavior?"

Vetoing that subject firmly, Grace said, "That's definitely conversation best saved for when we know each other better, Mr. Lazur—"

"Luke. Well, at least we're talking about getting to know each other better. This is further than I've gotten with a woman in years, let me tell you!" He spun on his chair and shoved his empty glass across the bar.

"I can't believe that," Grace chided mildly. "Not after having seen the way women watch you."

"Huh?" He looked at her and blinked, apparently not understanding.

"In the airport," Grace responded, foolishly proud that she had unwound enough to speak so frankly with a complete stranger. "Except in the movies, I'd never actually seen a woman undress a man with her eyes until just a few minutes ago."

He folded his hands on the bar like a schoolboy who'd been called on by the teacher. Meekly, he guessed, "The girl in the tight blue jeans?"

Grace couldn't stop her grin. "And I thought you hadn't noticed." Her voice was light.

"Of course I noticed. Under normal circumstances, I might have tried to do something about that look in her eye.

But not with you along. You're much more interesting, as a matter of fact, even if you do look at me like I'm a laboratory animal."

"I do not!" Grace exclaimed, startled by his observation.

"No? How many pro ball players do you know who don't spit chewing tobacco and scratch—"

"All right, all right," Grace intervened quickly before he embarrassed her. "Perhaps I am judging you. You're a new experience for me, I admit. Please excuse me if I've made you uncomfortable."

"I'm not uncomfortable. I guess I should have shaved, though." He rubbed his rough chin with his palm, his hauntingly heavy eyes resting thoughtfully on Grace as he spoke his mind. "I'm as intrigued as you are. You're just as unique to me as I am to you, y'know. How about another drink?"

Grace hadn't realized how quickly she'd downed her gimlet. This kind of talk had caused her to let down her guard, and she wasn't sure of herself at the moment. Not only was Luke a stunning example of masculinity, but he was needling her, too. However, he was doing it gently enough to keep her from marching out the door. It wasn't a scary feeling that had begun to assert itself in the recesses of her stomach—in fact, it was a rather exhilarating one. It had been too long since Grace had flirted with an available man.

Becoming blunt once more, she asked, "Is this customary in Pittsburgh? A gentleman buys too many drinks, gets the lady to talk about personal subjects calculated to throw her off balance, and then repeats the invitation to adjourn to the ever-popular 'my place' until she gives in?"

"It's a timeless technique used throughout the civilized world," Luke explained, pretending great seriousness as for an intellectual subject. He planted his elbow on the bar and smiled at her. "I'm not especially good at it, though, just quick with the smart-aleck remarks. Besides, the drinks were free. Have I got you off-balance?"

"A little, yes."

"You're not starting to think about birth control yet, are you?"

"Ooh, goodness," Grace said under her breath, trying not to look flustered.

He laughed. "Relax. I'm not asking. In fact, most women don't wait for men to make the first move anymore. I'm getting shell-shocked, I think. Have you any idea what pressure does to a guy like me?"

"I can guess," Grace said dryly.

"I bet you'd guess wrong," he said with a laugh. "Just relax. This is kind of nice for once. We both need a change, I think. You've been on top of a pedestal too long."

"My friend Lucy would certainly agree." Grace said, swishing the lime twist in her glass.

Luke nodded once, watching her measuringly. "Lucy was right—about your coming out here and having a look around at the rest of us, I mean."

"Oh? What's your theory?"

He gave a slight shrug. "Maybe Lucy felt you needed a change of scenery in more ways than one. Etiquette can be a different bag of tricks in different settings."

"No, no..." Grace began immediately, rising to the argument. She was usually prepared to wrangle until her opponent gave up in exhaustion. But it was senseless to start another variation of the same discussion tonight with Luke. She had a plane to catch, of course. Despite her absurd wish to stay exactly where she was and drink and chat for the next hour while a horrid little airplane made its bumpy way to Cleveland, Grace knew she had to leave. Better to part company now before this deceptively honest and attractive Luke Lazurnovich developed any ideas about pressing his luck. She explained herself by merely saying "That's a sore subject with me and always has been. I wish we had time to discuss it completely. But..."

When Grace reached for her gloves once more. Luke didn't protest. He watched her for another moment, however, with a half-smile on his mouth; she didn't try to guess what he was thinking. After having noted her signs of departure, he reached for her attaché case and handed it into her grasp. Without protest, he got to his feet like a mountain lion that had been lazing in the sun. Grace couldn't help noticing. He left the five-dollar bill on the bar, even though the bartender had said the drinks were on the house.

He took up her luggage and they went out into the airport together once more.

"Thank you for the drink," Grace told him as she settled her coat over her arm again. "And for the entertaining conversation."

"Not sparkling, huh? Just entertaining."

Grace smiled and relented, saying, "It was most pleasant. Thank you."

"Anytime. It wasn't bad for me, either. I guess I expected to you correct my grammar or something."

"I didn't notice that it needed correction," Grace said mildly as they strolled together along the long stretch of airport concourse. The crowd wasn't as bad as it had been a few minutes before, but Grace barely noticed that. Luke Lazurnovich had captivated her attention. Even if all the other women in sight hadn't been so obvious in their admiration, Grace would have realized that Luke was, in the vernacular, a very sexy guy. His walk alone, a slight saunter with just a hint of a casual roll, drew the appreciative female eye. And he hadn't turned out to be a mindless goon in the body of a god. She said honestly, "You've been good company when I needed it, and I *have* appreciated your help. I'm not nearly as nervous as I was when we got here. You're actually very sensitive, aren't you?"

"We'll see what you have to say about that," he predicted, "after you've had breakfast in my kitchen."

"I think I'll forgo that pleasure," Grace said with a laugh as they arrived at the bank of television sets once more. She extended her hand for him to shake and prepared to say good-bye.

"I don't think you'll forgo anything," Luke disagreed, looking over her head at the blinking television screens. "Except a flight to Cleveland."

Grace spun around in dismay. "Oh, no!"

"Canceled," Luke read aloud, sounding far from sorry. "See? Cleveland's closed. So are Buffalo and Youngstown. You're grounded, Princess."

"Oh, damn!"

He laughed in delight. "Hey, is that what Dear Ms. Barrett says in polite company?"

"Damn and blast! Now what?" Grace demanded, infuriated. "I'm supposed to be on a talk show there tomorrow afternoon!"

Luke reached and took her elbow in one of his big hands. His fingers didn't close around her slim arm, but he cupped her loosely and used his leverage to turn her away from the televisions, drawing her out of the mainstream of traffic and into an alcove below a motionless escalator. "Don't lose your cool now, Princess Grace," he coached. "That drink got you nicely simmered down, but I don't think you want another one. Not before you eat something."

"This is so maddening!" Grace cried, slapping her gloves against her thigh.

"I'm sure," Luke said sympathetically. "Well? How about it? My place?"

Grace pulled her arm from his grasp and faced him, still feeling angry. "Of course not. Thank you, but I couldn't. I'm sure I'll manage to find—"

"Honestly," he said with patience, "you're not going to find a room, and it would be hell to wander around here all night, waiting for Cleveland to open again. Think. You may as well come with me."

"I couldn't. Can't. Thank you, but—"

Luke dropped both her suitcases on the floor with a double thud and interrupted. "I know, I know, we haven't been properly introduced."

He took a step and bowed at an invisible person beside him and then to Grace. In an imitation of a highbrow New England accent, he said, "Miss Grace Barrett, may I have the *pleasure* of introducing His *Royal* Highness Lucius Baines Lazurnovich, Emperor of the Kingdom of the Lateral Sweep from the Forty-Yard Line and heir to the throne of the Football Hall of Fame? Your Highness, this is Miss Barrett, of the publishing Barretts—not the Barretts in *trade*, of course. Surely you've heard of them? How do you *do*, Miss Barrett? Have we met before perhaps? The south of France?

Aren't the beaches quite *dazzling* this time of year?"

A sputter of laughter escaped Grace's mouth just before she clapped her hand there to smother her reaction. He was hilarious.

"There. See?" he demanded, his eyes flashing. "Painless. Now, let's go before we both get stranded here for the night. I'm starving." He grabbed up her bags to emphasize his determination.

"Mr. Lazurnavich, please, it's really very kind of you—"

"Luke. Just Luke. It's easy to say and only one syllable." He was losing his temper. "I'm *hungry*, dammit! Can't we go? I'm not asking you to sleep with me, for godsake."

"Oh, dear," Grace muttered, covering her eyes with her hand in dismay. Did he mean it? Really? Surely, he'd come on to her if he got the chance. Perhaps he meant to soften her up—put her off her guard with false assurances and then get her in the mood so he could have his way with her later.

"Relax. I'm not the raping kind. Your royal virtue is a darn sight safer with me than it would be in Cleveland! Come on."

Grace took a step after him uncertainly, moaning, "Oh, dear . . ."

"Come *on*," he insisted with exasperation. "Haven't you ever heard what starving football players are like? Move it, lady!"

By that time, he was already striding purposefully for the nearest exit, and Grace realized she'd better keep up or lose her luggage completely. She made a dash for it and caught up just as he was stowing her bags in the back seat of the snow-covered limo. He popped open the front passenger door and indicated she ought to jump in there before he went around the hood of the car and began to argue with the cop who was calmly writing out a ticket in the middle of the blizzard. Grace ducked into the car, gasping to control her breath and her runaway imagination. Grace Barrett railroaded into spending the night with a football player? What was the world coming to?

Luke lost the argument with cop, accepted the ticket with surprising good grace, and climbed in behind the wheel. His mood was light, in spite of the ticket, but when he drove the car out onto the highway again, he concentrated on avoiding an accident. Grace was grateful that he drove sensibly. From her seat in the front of the car, she could see how treacherous the road was. She kept quiet.

Dear Ms. Barrett,
   What does a young woman do when she discovers she's agreed to a one-night stand and has second thoughts almost right away? Please hurry with your response!
      —Can't Wait Much Longer in Louisiana

Dear Lou,
   You have two choices: Either get out of the car and walk home, or take your medicine like a big girl.

New York was too far to walk tonight, and besides, this wasn't really a one-night stand. At least, she *hoped* it wasn't.

Luke's house was in a nearby suburb, she discovered. He drove along an almost deserted commercial street—past a restaurant, a grocery, and a pharmacy—before ducking into a driveway alongside a large garage and parking lot. LASER'S JAGUARS read the sign that was swinging madly in the wind. A pickup truck was buried beneath a blanket of snow under the street lamp.

The drive ran along a high wooden fence and finally ended outside a split-level house with an oversize garage. Luke drove the limo as close to a side entrance as he could get and then shut off the engine. He hauled her suitcases over the seat and got out into the storm. Grace followed suit, and in less than a minute they were safely out of the wind and inside a cold but quiet garage. Two cars were parked there, but in the darkness Grace didn't take notice of them except to see that the hoods were both up to allow tinkering underneath.

"This way," Luke directed, threading his way between

the cars and heading for another door. He pushed through and called, "Watch your feet. I had to fire the butler for hassling the upstairs maid."

They trooped through a darkened laundry room, the floor of which was littered with boots and shoes and what looked like a discarded pair of coveralls, a basketball, as well as the expected football, a broken hockey stick, and what might have been a shotgun hanging by its trigger guard on a hook over the dryer, except that Grace saw the name BUBBLE BLASTER written in fluorescent yellow letters along the barrel. This room was apparently Luke Lazurnovich's toy chest.

Grace picked her way cautiously through the mess and asked, "I realize that this is a belated question, but have you any children, Mr. Laser?"

"Not that I know of," he said from the stairway. "At least, I haven't run across any recently. I haven't been down to the basement lately, though. This way. Watch your head."

Grace ducked under his arm and crossed the threshold into the kitchen. Behind her, Luke flipped on a light switch.

His kitchen was clean—a little cluttered perhaps, but not an appalling mess. It was *L*-shaped, with a breakfast table tucked into a corner by the window and two bow-backed maple armchairs abandoned haphazardly nearby. He'd left a coffee mug on the table beside a folded newspaper. An empty milk carton stood in the sink, but there were no dirty dishes. He wasn't a slob, at least.

The cheery vinyl floor was spotless, and so were the windows. There were no frilly curtains, just a set of matchstick blinds that looked serviceable as well as arty. Nor were there decorations on the walls except a clock, and the absence of a cutesy set of canisters stacked on the countertop confirmed Grace's belief that Luke Lazurnovich was a bachelor. A woman would have succumbed to temptation and decorated the overhead beams, the bowed window, and the empty white wall in the popular country-look clutter. Grace was almost relieved to find that Luke hadn't scattered cheap antiques all over the place.

"The living room's that way, and here's a bathroom." He pushed a doorway open with his boot and headed around the corner with her luggage, saying over his shoulder, "Look around, if you like. You can put your coat in the closet to your left."

He was taking her suitcases upstairs and politely giving her an opportunity to use the bathroom, Grace decided. After hanging up her coat, she took him up on the offer and sequestered herself in the small lavatory off the kitchen for a few minutes. It gave her time to think.

Unfortunately, she wasn't thinking very straight. At all costs, however, she decided she was going to have to take the upper hand and prevent the evening from turning into a sordid one-night sexual encounter. Heavens, not Grace Barrett!

Luke thudded down the stairs soon afterward and made a beeline for the refrigerator. He was calmly unfastening the top few buttons on his flannel shirt and studying the possibilities when Grace joined him. Without turning around to her, he said, "There's sandwich stuff or eggs and bacon. I'm not much for breakfast at night, but you're welcome to fix whatever you like."

"A sandwich would help, I'm sure," Grace said, and she unfastened the silver buttons on her snug-fitting gray wool jacket. "What can I do to help?"

He was lining up an assortment of packages on the counter by the toaster—lettuce, cheese, meat, and tomatoes—but he pointed above her head. "Bread's up there. Chips, too. And I'm crazy for Lorna Doones. See the package? There's milk or beer or ginger ale. Or coffee. What would you like?"

"Ginger ale sounds good." Grace laid her jacket over the nearest chair and stretched for the cupboard he had indicated. She found whole-wheat bread and a depleted loaf of rye, along with a bag of slightly squished butter cookies and a bag of semi-crumbled corn chips. She added those items to his growing pile and stood back to unbutton the sleeves of her blouse and roll them up.

Luke closed the refrigerator with his hip and turned, a jar of mustard and a larger one of mayonnaise in his hands. He hesitated.

Grace finished rolling up the right sleeve of her shell-pink silk blouse and realized that Luke was staring. Well, not staring exactly, but looking startled.

He collected himself immediately. "Uh, that's pretty. I didn't—I mean, you look different without your jacket."

Her suit was tailored and trim, pearl gray in color and probably a bit stiff-looking. Grace knew that her slim but womanly figure looked best if it was encased in classic lines, but she usually softened the look with a pastel blouse underneath. Her buttoned-up jacket must have seemed quite severe. This blouse was loose across her breasts, which were full and curving without making her look like Dolly Parton's clone, and the delicately snug ruffle at her throat tickled her slightly pointed chin when she turned her head. Pale pink was her best color, for it softened the cornsilk blondness of her hair and enhanced her own naturally pink cheekbones. It was a very feminine blouse and was probably prettier than Luke had expected. His look said it all. Until now, he hadn't really noticed how female she was.

Grace was stung by his lack of interest in her appearance. He didn't find her attractive! He was a clod after all! Maybe the girl in the tight blue jeans had caught his eye in the airport, but he hadn't cared a whit for Grace's very expensive and meticulously tailored outfit!

"Very pretty," he said again, sounding bland. He put the mustard down and began to undo the twist tie on the bread.

Of course, Grace had been perfectly aware of his size and general shape, but when Luke Lazurnovich turned his back to her and began to make his supper, she suddenly took inventory of his various physical attributes.

He was enormous, to begin with, not just tall and broad through the shoulders. His back was very long and tapered as if deliberately sculpted to such perfection. His disreputable corduroy trousers clung with a comfortable snugness to his hips before loosening around the more taut muscles of his behind and hard, curving thighs. Weren't wide receivers also runners? Luke looked as if he hadn't stopped training yet. And he moved with the sure grace of a wild animal, or perhaps a dancer. Yes, that was it. He was conscious of his body, yet not aware of the fluid way he used it. Standing at the kitchen counter, with his weight resting casually on one leg while the other rested gently against the cupboards below, he looked relaxed and confident.

Nuts to you, Luke the Laser, Grace groused inwardly. So he didn't think she was as much of a woman as the chick in the blue jeans, hm? Well, a different kind of female might try to show him otherwise, but Grace was not going to lower herself. At all costs, Grace Barrett maintained her cool, refined, and gracious composure.

She finished rolling her other sleeve and joined him, taking a moment to wash her hands at the tap. She kept her tone well modulated and courteous as she remarked, "Suddenly, I'm quite hungry."

"Fend for yourself," Luke replied, sending a grin down at her that taunted her oh-so-sophisticated tone. He said, "I haven't eaten since noon, and it's fight for survival around here."

"Move over, buster," she commanded lightly, giving him a little bump with her hip and giving up her hauteur. He seemed pretty safe so far.

He shifted, and they stood together, building sandwiches and making small talk about the food. Luke pulled a pair of glasses from a shelf and passed Grace a bottle of ginger ale. He poured himself a tall glass of milk, drank half of it down, then filled the glass again before returning the carton to the fridge. Next, he measured coffee and dumped it into a paper filter while Grace filled the pot from the tap. He turned on the coffee maker and then carried his plate into the next room. Grace followed. This was not a formal dinner with five kinds of wine and demitasse spoons, she noted.

His living room was furnished with a mishmash of pieces that Grace realized immediately were several years old, but of good quality indeed. There was one antique, a desk in the far corner—the kind Grace remembered seeing in paintings of the young Ben Franklin—but it didn't clash with the modern lines of two tuxedo sofas upholstered in a rich chocolate-colored rough cotton. There was a comfortably cluttered air about the room, with magazines overflowing their racks and a few days' worth of mail scattered on the trestle-type coffee table. A pair of very large running shoes had been abandoned under the desk. Being a neat person by nature, Grace felt an automatic urge to line them up side by side, but she refrained.

A slipcovered armchair and footstool stood under a brass floor lamp, and Luke headed for that. He remembered himself in time, though, and instead led his guest to the pair of sofas in front of the fireplace. While Grace sat down on the first, balancing her supper on her knees, Luke put his oversize plate on the opposite sofa and went to crouch before the hearth. He struck a long kitchen match and tinkered with a gas lever, and in a moment a whoosh of flame sprang up around some cut lengths of wood that had already been laid in the grate. The room was suddenly cozy.

While he dusted off his hands, Grace glanced around the room to try to gauge Luke's personality by the things he kept. Perhaps he had once made a halfhearted attempt at decorating the place, for a watercolor painting, a summer landscape done in vivid hues of green and gold, had been propped on the mantel. He hadn't found the time to hang it properly, Grace decided. The place looked lived in, yet it lacked the touches that would make it a well-*loved* home. The cozy, crackling fire was deceptive. This was Luke's house, but he wasn't emotionally attached to it.

The painting drew Grace's attention a moment longer. It was a pretty thing, actually. Not cutesy or painfully detailed, but rather a nice bit of artwork. Surely Luke hadn't chosen such a picture. The landscape was too subtle for him. Perhaps this was a sign that he had indeed been domesticated at one time. Had Luke been married? A semiattractive man his age usually didn't make it past thirty without being married at least once.

Deciding it was time to find out, Grace cleared her throat and observed, "That's a very nice picture. Did you find it locally?"

Luke was about to sit down, but he followed her gaze as if he'd forgotten what picture she might be talking about. "What? That? I don't know where she got it, to tell you the truth."

"She?" Grace inquired politely.

Luke measured her with a steady look. "My ex-wife. That was her favorite picture, but when the movers took her stuff out of here, I substituted another picture for that and kept it."

"A bullfighter on black velvet?"

Luke laughed and sat down. "I think it was a bare-breasted Spanish lady with eyes like Bambi, as a matter of fact. A holdover from my college days. It bore a remarkable resemblance to my wife, and she hated it. My final revenge, you could say, for a long and rather unpleasant marriage."

"I see," Grace murmured, and she picked up her sandwich to avoid continuing the obvious conversation. Discussing a man's ex-wife was did not exist in the realm of proper behavior.

Luke relaxed, untying his boots and kicking them off before reclining on the opposite sofa with the air of a man about to enjoy his meal without a trace of good manners. Putting his milk within easy reach, he squished his first sandwich with his palm so that it wouldn't fall apart when he picked it up. Then he popped a Lorna Doone cookie into his mouth and crunching it, asked bluntly, "You married?"

He was acting as if he didn't care one way or the other, Grace noted with a twinge of resentment. It was obvious that Luke the Laser did not consider a woman like Grace Barrett to be a *real* woman in whom *real* men might be interested. She was sexless to him. With asperity, she lifted her nose and said, "No, as a matter of fact, I am not."

He took a huge chomp out of his sandwich and nodded, as if that response made perfect sense. Of course not, he seemed to say. It's understandable. Who would marry a stuffy dame like you?

Grace considered his attitude while they ate in silence. Perhaps he was right. She *was* stuffy, and perhaps overly cold sometimes. Grace supposed she had several reasons for acting the way she did, the first and foremost being that she was the offspring of the famous Caroline Barrett, dowager of American etiquette. But Grace's attitude toward the opposite sex had not been molded by her mother. Grace had come to put a distance between herself and men for her own reasons.

It was Kip, she supposed, and her relationship with him that had caused her to be so cool and stiff with men these days. A ridiculous name, Kip, but Kenworth Ivan Peers sounded even worse. Kip had been his name since prep school, when they'd first met.

It was a short story, Grace realized, although it had spanned nearly half her life. She and Kip had met at dancing class in New York. Terribly highbrow, of course, but it was the truth. He'd been about to start Choate, and she'd been two years younger. They were the same breed, from the same kind of aristocratic stock. They'd been companions at first, and after ten years—yes, *ten*—they had become lovers. An engagement took place on schedule after Kip got an important promotion as a commodities broker. The marriage had been planned but had never taken place. Grace sampled her first of Luke the Laser's corn curls thoughtfully. The wedding should have been performed two months ago, and yet, she could hardly muster any sadness now.

The problem had arisen when Grace's mother resigned as Dear Mrs. Barrett. Grace had changed the syndicated column to Dear Ms. Barrett and had begun her own career. Kip had not been amused. In fact, her success annoyed him. He resented her sudden celebrity, although he'd enjoyed her mother's fame. Oddly enough, their sex life had reflected his emotional state before anything else. Kip had developed a potency problem that infuriated him to no end and finally caused their breakup. The psychologist whom Grace had visited a few times told her that subconsciously Kip was punishing her for her success by withholding the intimacy that she longed for most, but Grace hadn't believed that distasteful theory. And she hadn't gone back to hear more.

It had taken nearly six months, but Grace felt strong again now. She'd had her whole life woven neatly with Kip's, and suddenly to be the object of his resentment had been difficult. She hadn't seen him since autumn, and he'd been quite rude then. She had learned to go about her life's business without him.

Grace eyed Luke the Laser as he swallowed the last bite of his second sandwich and licked a trace of mayonnaise from his thumb. She'd wager *he* didn't have a potency problem. She began to wonder just what kind of woman got Luke interested.

Dear Ms. Barrett,
*   What does a young lady do when she's attracted to a young man and he doesn't know she exists?*
*   —Unrequited in Utah*

Dear Unrequited,
*   Unrequited love is beyond my expertise. Check with Abby.*

CHAPTER THREE

AN HOUR LATER, Grace wondered why a civilized woman should feel insulted if a man didn't make a pass at her.

Luke gathered their plates and saw to washing up the dishes, and then he said good night to her and gave her directions to the guest room. He went up the stairs, and a moment later she heard a door close. Yes, she thought, she was insulted. Grace knew that her friend Lucy would have ended the evening quite differently. Not that Grace *wanted* to sleep with Luke the Laser, but—well, wasn't an attempt on his part at least in order? Perhaps she'd been out of the mainstream too long. She rinsed out her coffee cup and went up to bed herself.

The guest room was pretty but bare. There were two twin beds covered with white eyelet spreads, a maple dresser with a mirror perfect for stashing snapshots, and a desk with a study lamp. No pictures on the walls, no little girl paraphernalia to mark this as a room that anyone used with any regularity. An adjoining bathroom was very clean, which led Grace to believe that Luke the Laser had a cleaning lady.

He'd left her suitcases on one of the beds, and Grace puttered for a while, unpacking her toilet articles and hanging clothes for the next day on the shower curtain rod. Thoughts of the man in the next room filled her head as she worked. Not only had she found his body and his easy way of moving a delight to watch, but she had also found him rather entertaining. It annoyed her that the feeling wasn't mutual.

If Luke the Laser had been recently divorced, she could understand his disinterest in the opposite sex. But this house hadn't seen a female hand in years. There was no explanation for his complete lack of interest in her except that Luke Lazurnovich just didn't find Grace Barrett attractive. As Lucy would say, she didn't turn him on.

She ought to be pleased to discover that he was a gentleman, she argued with herself, feeling plaintive. She undressed and showered, then slipped into a Victorian-style pink nightgown complete with long sleeves, a lace collar, and a bustlelike gathering of material just below the curve of her lower back. It was Grace's usual night apparel—not sexy, of course, but comfortable, and certainly pretty. Grace supposed that Luke the Laser preferred women in black nylon peekaboos. She got into the bed and stewed. How come she was feeling so angry with him?

To the slowly diminishing noise of the blizzard, Grace went to sleep and didn't awaken until morning.

Dear Ms. Barrett,

    When should a houseguest descend for breakfast when it appears that the host is going to sleep very late?

                  —No Breakfast in
                      New Brunswick

Dear No,

    You have two choices: You may starve yourself, thereby leaving a ghastly mess for your host when he finally arises; or you may wait until you hear water running elsewhere in the house and then go down-

stairs. It's quite acceptable for you to make your own breakfast, for some hosts even appreciate such self-reliance.

Grace usually took her own advice. But by nine o'clock she hadn't heard a sound in Luke the Laser's house except for her own stomach's grumbling, so she buttoned her dressing gown up around her throat and tiptoed down to the kitchen for something to eat. She made a fresh pot of coffee and two slices of whole-wheat toast for herself, and had just sat down at the table to trim off the crusts, when she heard a thump and crash from the laundry room. She sat very still and waited.

Another thud, and then Luke himself came catapulting up the stairs two at a time. Evidently, he'd been outside already. He burst through the door, breathing hard, and came up short, his startled blue eyes wide upon seeing Grace. "Oh!"

Grace composedly finished trimming her toast, and said with a regal lift of her nose, "Good morning. I thought you were still asleep."

"Uh, no. I get up at six," he said, trying to calm his labored breathing and collect his dignity.

It wasn't easy. He was dressed in a shapeless, tattered gray outfit that was called—in certain athletic circles that Grace generally avoided—a sweat suit. And he was certainly perspiring. He'd been out running, she guessed by the sopping condition of his shoes and the soaked state of the yellow-and-black-striped terry-cloth strip he wore clasped around his head to hold his hair out of his eyes and absorb the rivulets that threatened to endanger his vision. He had a set of headphones clamped over his ears and was listening to music from a tiny transistor radio that was clipped to his shorts. He took off the headphones immediately.

Grace looked him up and down and decided on a suitable caption: *The Hulk in All His Splendor*. Luke the Laser looked magnificently male. Like an idiot, Grace dropped her knife with a clatter.

Without a trace of a smirk, Luke crossed to the sink in

three graceful strides and turned on the tap full blast. He cupped his hands and bent forward to slosh the water over his face and down his neck, all the while shuddering at the shock of the cold water on his skin. Grace watched covertly. His baggy pants skimmed his hips, then stretched tightly to reveal the muscular curve of his backside. The white rim of his underwear showed above the waistband of the pants, and then a four-inch gap of golden skin gleamed with a sheen of perspiration before disappearing into the top of his shirt. The sinewy lengths of his thighs were just a suggestion under the thick insulation of clothing, but the tendons behind his knees and the lanky muscles of his calves were easily discernible and rather nice to look at—shaped for severest exercise, yet supremely beautiful. Grace suspected that his upper body was just as well defined, just as— Good grief, she was ogling again! She took a swift, vicious bite of her toast and looked away.

Luke finished washing up, pulling off the headband and tossing it on the counter. Then he reached for the dish towel and dried his face without turning around.

She'd better not let him see how entranced she was by his appearance. Grace pushed aside the unpleasant thought that he might intend to dry dishes with the very same towel that he was using on himself, and cleared her throat. Smoothly, she said, "I took the liberty of making toast for myself. Shall I make some for you?"

"No, thanks. I'll have fruit or something. You okay this morning?" He turned around and leaned against the counter to look down at her. The shapeless shirt hung loosely around his midsection, but clung damply to his shoulders and collarbones. The stain of sweat was dark across his chest.

The Beast, Grace decided, was a better caption. Was he trying to shock her? she wondered. Surely that gleam in his eyes belied his casual stance before her. Was he teasing her with his resplendent masculinity? Grace attempted a polite smile and hoped he didn't see that he was succeeding in blowing her cool. She replied, "Very well, thank you. I haven't called the airport yet, however."

Luke looked her over for a moment. He must be accus-

tomed to having female guests for breakfast, but the longer
he surveyed her there, the more he seemed mystified by the
sedate, ladylike picture she made sitting at his table. Grace
pretended she didn't notice his frank attention. With an odd
smile, he studied her powder-blue velour dressing gown
with its embroidered violets and matching satin slippers. He
noted the way she'd pinned her blond hair carefully on the
crown of her head, and the graceful movements of her hands
as she nibbled the corner of her toast. Suddenly, he smiled
for real, as if amused by her appearance. Then he tossed
the frilly towel over his shoulder and headed for the refrigerator. *"I* called the airport. Cleveland's open. There's a
flight at ten-thirty."

"Oh," Grace murmured uneasily. She put down her wedge
of toast as a knot of tension filled her stomach. Thoughts
of airplanes were not her favorite way to start the day. Her
fear of flying had evaporated while her head was full of
Luke the Laser's physical beauty, but now it came back
with an awful rush. Her flight to Cleveland loomed like a
black thundercloud, and she paled.

"Hmm," said Luke, noting her reaction with a sidelong
look. "I thought you'd be pleased, after last night."

Grace met his gaze and blinked. "Last night?"

He ducked his head into the refrigerator and said care-
lessly, "Yeah. Staying here, I mean. This isn't exactly the
Hilton. You didn't look very happy once we got here."

"I—" Grace floundered for a moment. "I apologize.
You've been most hospitable. I'm afraid, well, I wasn't
very pleasant company last night. Please excuse me."

Luke straightened to his full height, casually tossing a
grapefruit from one hand to the other like a juggler. "I
figured you were overwhelmed."

"By the airport? Yes, a little."

"No," he contradicted. "By me and this place. I'm not
exactly Gary Cooper in a suave double-breasted suit. Do
you want some grapefruit?"

"No, no, thank you," Grace said quickly. "Honestly,
Mr. Lazur—I mean Luke, you've been charming and very

gracious, and I appreciate what you've done. I just—"

"Don't say you're sorry," he instructed, going to the sink purposefully. He pulled a small knife from a rack there and began to cut into the fruit he held in his left hand. Juice spurted out, spraying the already damp front of his shirt, but he didn't appear to notice. He set down the knife and said, "Look, we're from two different worlds. You're allowed to be a little overwhelmed. Heck, I was, too. But it was interesting. For me, I mean. I've never spent much time around anyone like you."

"I see," Grace said weakly. He wasn't exactly heaping her with compliments. He was also peeling off the skin of the grapefruit with a technique Grace recognized from an old movie about Henry VIII—plenty of juice dripping off his fingers and a clear intention of gobbling down the food without benefit of utensils or anything resembling a napkin. The grapefruit looked like a small tangerine in his big hand and he was treating it just that way, stripping off the skin in preparation for eating it in sections. Suddenly, a squirt of juice shot out from between Luke's fingers, landing squarely in Grace's eye. She gasped and grabbed for her napkin.

"You're nice," Luke added, not noticing as Grace clutched her smarting eye. "You didn't make me feel like a mannerless bumpkin."

The fact was, however, that he *was* eating his breakfast like an ill-mannered oaf. Grace moved back to avoid getting squirted again and decided that, on behalf of her own delicate sensibilites, she shouldn't watch his operation on the grapefruit. She concentrated on her dry toast for a moment. "Thank you. I can— I'll just finish my breakfast and dress and call a cab. You may have your house to yourself again in a short while."

"Umm," Luke agreed. The peeling operation completed, he came to the table and pushed the other chair out with his foot. Then he sat down across from Grace and put both his elbows on the table. He was absolutely enormous. His dark hair, damp from his exertions as well as the sink-splashing, clung in handsome curls around his slim head.

With a jolt of surprise, Grace realized that he'd shaved. His cheeks were smooth, and the small cleft in his chin looked neat and handsome. What had prompted him to do it? What did this courtesy signify? Grace couldn't begin to guess. She eyed him warily, and Luke began to pull apart the grapefruit with a tantalizing slowness that she decided must have been calcuated. He had to be flaunting his crudeness, right?

Luke seemed unware of his uncivilized behavior and lifted his head to study Grace for a moment. "You know," he said briskly, "if you don't take this the wrong way, I've got a suggestion."

He was sensually barbaric. Mesmerized by the bare-handed way he thrust his thumb down into the grapefruit, sectioned it, and swallowed the first bite whole, Grace knew her inquiry was unsteady. "A suggestion?"

He gulped and nodded, and with the back of his hand he caught the first dribble of juice before it left his mouth. "Sure," he said easily. "Why don't I take you?"

Grace stared. "What? You mean to the airport or—?"

"No, no. To Cleveland." His blue eyes met hers directly. "I'll drive you up."

"Drive me? No, I couldn't— No, it's—"

He brushed aside her hasty blundering and said, "The weather's beautiful—couldn't be better. The roads are terrific and the sun's out already. It'd be a gorgeous ride with the snow looking the way it does."

Grace objected. "Oh, that's impossible! You're very kind to offer, but I couldn't possibly—"

"Think about it," Luke said, concentrating on his fruit. He tore off another section and popped it into his mouth. Around it, he said, "No airplane ride."

That logic did make Grace pause. The one thing in life that truly terrified her was getting on an airplane. Just thinking about it made her stomach turn over.

"But if you really don't mind flying," Luke continued casually, teasing her, "I suppose you could catch that plane this morning. It's a quick flight, of course. Hardly enough time to get settled in your seat. Just up," he explained, making an airplane of his hand and zooming it up toward the ceiling, "and down again."

"All right," Grace said, shuddering when his hand did a crash landing on the table between them. She met his eyes and knew hers were uncertain. Which was worse—dying in a plane crash or spending more time with the Incredible Hulk?

He smiled at her, trying to translate her response. "All right?"

"Are you serious?" Grace asked curiously, unwilling to trust the twinkle in his eyes. He'd been perfectly safe, after all. There hadn't been a sordid scene last night, for better or for worse. Or worse? Good heavens! Grace realized that she was actually *interested* in this man! It just went to prove that hormones could occasionally get the better of an ingrained way of civilized life. Could it be true? Was some primitive alter ego inside herself actually attracted in some uncouth way to this man?

"I'm serious," Luke said.

"Why?" Grace blurted out, unthinking. "I mean—"

His grin broadened and he passed her a section of his grapefruit. "I don't mind. I've got some parts to deliver up there anyway. I'll shower and be dressed in fifteen minutes."

"Luke—" Grace objected, taking the fruit from him without thinking. The way she'd said his name sounded odd to her, almost too intimate, as if their relationship were much different suddenly. Grace stopped uncertainly at the thought. What was she getting into?

He shook his head, his mouth full again. "I don't mind, really. I'll get a kick out of it. You're not bad company, y'know."

His taunt was obvious. Collecting herself, Grace gave him a wry sideways look and demanded, "Are you looking at me as if I were a laboratory animal?"

Luke polished off his breakfast and, smiling, admitted, "Sure. You're better-looking than most. You look great this

morning, in fact, like you've just had a bath and you're still
a little drowsy. Your face looks like a child's, and I love
your mouth."

Grace blinked at him in stunned surprise. "I thought
you—I mean—"

"That I hadn't noticed?" Luke pushed himself away from
the table with a laugh. "I noticed. You're lovely when you
aren't acting like Cleopatra in a truss."

Annoyed, Grace glared at his back while he went to the
sink to rinse the juice off his hands. "I realize that I might
be a bit chilly from time to time—"

"Chilly? Princess, you're Frigidaire's biggest competition!" Luke dried his hands on the towel again and faced
her. "I'm intimidated as hell, in fact, and hardly in a position
to try thawing you out a little. Eat your breakfast and get
dressed."

"Let me reimburse you for your trouble, then. I'm on
an expense account, of course, and you're certainly entitled
to some sort of payment for—"

"Forget it. We're leaving in fifteen minutes."

"Fifteen—!"

He tossed the towel at her as he went past the table, and
a moment later he bounded up the stairs for the shower. He
started to whistle in the upper hall.

Grace sat for a moment eyeing the dripping chunk of
grapefruit in her fingers.

Dear Ms. Barrett,
   *A local accountant has offered to help me prepare
my tax return this year, but he says he doesn't expect
me to pay for his services. What should I do?*
                            —Penniless in Pensacola

Dear Less,
   *Under no circumstances should you trust a man
who offers something for nothing. He'd be a fool not
to have an ulterior motive up his sleeve.*

What the heck, Grace thought. She popped the grapefruit

into her mouth and savored the acid sweetness. As she chewed the too-large mouthful, she speculated about Luke the Laser. Maybe a drive to Cleveland with him would be enlightening. In any case, it would be daringly different. Lucy would be proud of such impulsive behavior. It was occasionally revitalizing to do something new and daring. What the heck. Grace licked the juice from her fingers and got up. Ulterior motives could be dealt with.

Luke's garage specialized in Jaguars, Grace realized when they pulled away from his house and back down the alley to the street. He kept two of his own, and he had lovingly tinkered under the hood of this red beauty before he stowed her luggage in the small compartment behind the front seat. His own duffel-type bag didn't take up much space.

Grace settled into the plush leather seat with pleasure, enjoying the way the firm cushion conformed to her body. The Jaguar was a long, low convertible with a long, sensuous snout and a wonderful burbling engine that created a sexy kind of tremor in the car's frame as they sat briefly, waiting for a traffic light to change. The car had been equipped with an expensive-looking sound system and even a mobile telephone, which lay underneath the gear box. The steering wheel was thick and wrapped with fine black leather, and the numerous dials and switches on the dash glowed from polishing. It was the sort of car that men enjoyed driving, and Grace began to feel better about accepting Luke's offer. He looked happy behind the wheel, and had even pulled a jaunty plaid cap from the glove compartment and pulled it over his still-damp hair as he drove. Perhaps he had simply suggested the trip so that he'd have a chance to drive this handsome car.

And he didn't look so bad himself, for once. He'd showered and dressed in a remarkably adult-looking crew-neck sweater in a subtle—for him—canary yellow and a pair of almost new jeans that might even have been pressed. He'd brought along a wool-lined topcoat and an ancient Harris Tweed jacket, but he'd put them in the back to drive with freedom.

Grace had chosen her white wool trousers and matching short jacket with its double row of gold buttons. Her blouse was red, but the color only showed at the ruffled cuffs and the flowing bow at her throat. She had earrings to match and a red hat with a snappy brim that looked very stylish, if she could be allowed to say so herself. She'd made up her face impeccably and worn her hair swept up and clasped with pins, so that only tendrils showed behind her ears and from under her hat. On her feet Grace wore her suede boots again, but she'd tucked a pair of red heels into her attaché case to wear at the television station. Luke had not taken much time to absorb her outfit, but Grace sensed that he might have studied her briefly while she bent over to place her attaché case in the back seat.

The sunshine was glorious. And with the fresh accumulation of snow, the countryside looked marvelously clean and pretty. Grace snuggled back into the seat and enjoyed herself.

They talked. The conversation was mundane for a time, but gradually sought more personal ground.

"You get up very early," Grace noted when they had driven beyond the last suburb and headed into the country. "Is that habit, or some form of self-discipline?"

"Habit, I guess," Luke explained willingly. "I like mornings. Pretty today, isn't it?"

"Lovely," Grace agreed, although she was surprised to hear a man of his size and limited sophistication remark on the sights around them. She shrugged to herself and added happily, "I feel as if we should be taking a horse and sleigh."

"That would be safer than a car in Cleveland," Luke agreed wryly. "No hubcaps to steal."

Grace laughed at him. "Why such a distaste for Cleveland? I think you've really got a grudge!"

"If you knew anything about football, you'd understand the rivalry," Luke said loftily, getting comfortable in his seat and watching the road. "And that's also where my ex-wife lives, as a matter of fact. With her new husband. A jerk," Luke added informatively. "He used to be with the Indians' front office."

"Indians? That's a team, isn't it?"

Luke grinned and shook his head, giving up. "Forget I mentioned it. Let's just hope we can get in and out of the city without mishap. Do you have the address of the station?"

"In my bag, yes. Do you want to see it?"

"Not yet."

Grace checked her wristwatch and thought. The mere mention of the television station got her mind on the subject of the book tour. If Lucy had tried to call the hotel in Cleveland where a room had been reserved, she'd know Grace hadn't made it. Lucy might be concerned.

Luke had noticed her glance at her watch. "Worried?" he asked. "It'll take less than two hours to get up there."

"I'm not worried about the time," Grace explained swiftly. "But my publicist might have tried calling me last night. I should check in with her today, I think."

Luke reached for the phone box and lifted the receiver. He handed it across. "So call. I won't listen."

Surprised, Grace accepted the phone. "Really? Can I?"

"Of course." He explained how to dial and fell silent while Grace collected some papers from her attaché case and made her call. The publisher's switchboard answered in just a few seconds, and Lucy picked up her phone just an instant later.

"Luce?" Grace asked, feeling a surge of delight as she heard her best friend's voice over the crackling connection. "Hi, it's Gray."

"There you are!" Lucy abandoned her cool, official tone of voice and demanded, "Gray, darling, where the hell have you been?"

"Such a mess," Grace explained, conscious that Luke couldn't exactly turn off his ears. He had to overhear at least her side of the conversation. "I was stranded in Pittsburgh, that's all. The Cleveland airport closed because of a storm."

Lucy laughed. "Any excuse not to fly! You planned that blizzard yourself, didn't you? Now what? Can you catch a train and get to the next stop on your tour?"

"I—well, I don't have to," Grace said. "I've caught a ride, you could say."

"What?"

"We're driving to Cleveland. It turns out that it's not too far away and—"

"Who's *we?*" Lucy interrupted immediately, sounding suspicious. "Gray, what have you done?"

"Nothing, nothing. Everything's quite smooth. I should get to the television station in plenty of time."

"Grace Barrett," Lucy said severely, "I want to know what's going on. You sound like you're down a well. Or do you have a crazed ax-murderer standing over your shoulder?"

Grace paused and said slowly, "Not exactly."

Lucy was silent for a moment, then Grace got the impression that her friend was pulling the receiver close to her mouth. Lucy asked curiously, "Are you alone?"

"No."

"I see!" Lucy exclaimed with fiendish relish. "Now I get the picture! Is it a man?"

Cautiously, Grace answered, "Y-yes."

"No kidding! Gray! You little *vixen!* What are you doing out there in the hinterlands, may I ask?"

"I'm fine," Grace said stiffly, wishing to heaven that she'd waited until they'd gotten to the station so she could use a private telephone. Luke was less than an arm's length away, so Grace shifted the receiver to her other ear.

"You *witch!*" Lucy was saying. "I can't believe it! Is he right there with you now?"

"Yes."

"Oh, my *Gawd!* This is so unlike you, Gray! Tell *all!* No, I suppose you can't. I'll ask yes and no questions, all right?"

"Lucy, please—"

"Don't use your mother's tone with me. Tell me now—is he gorgeous?"

Grace swallowed hard. There was no use arguing with Lucy Simons in any situation. Lucy was a bully and Grace had always been the weaker-willed of the two. Taking breath for courage, Grace admitted, "Well, yes, I suppose."

Lucy giggled in delight. "I love it! Just like grade school! Is he a hunk?"

"That's precisely the word, as a matter of fact," Grace said, trying to sound as if she were discussing a very serious subject.

"My *dear!* A stud!" Lucy crowed. "You didn't—? Last night? With this person did you . . . ?"

"No," Grace said firmly. Then she qualified, "Not exactly."

"Not *exactly?* What does *that* mean? Did you sleep with him or not?"

"No!"

"But you stayed with him somewhere?" Lucy pressed avidly. "Stranded together in the storm? Alone together? Battling the elements and your own breathless desire for each other?"

"That's too many questions at once, Lucy."

"Good grief. You, of all people! Is he rich?"

"I haven't the faintest idea." Grace glanced without thinking at Luke's averted profile. He was paying attention to the road, thank heaven. She relented, saying, "Perhaps a little, though."

"And he's driving you today? In a spectacular car, I hope?"

"Yes, as a matter of fact," Grace said primly.

"A Rolls!" Lucy guessed in excitement.

"No. Please do not let your imagination get too far out of control, Lucille."

"Of course not, Gray!" Lucy was undaunted, full of energy and impulsive exclamations, as usual. "But you must call me back when you can and give me all the gory details! *Are* you going to sleep with him?"

"Lucy . . ." Grace warned.

"My dear, experience life! Forget your troubles and your mother and silly old Kip and —"

"I'd prefer to leave Kip out of this, all right?"

"Kip, Kip, Kip," Lucy snapped with annoyance. "Forget him. He was terrible in bed, anyway, right?"

"I should *never* have confided in you, Lucy!" Grace cried, covering her eyes with her hand in embarrassment.

"Well, I'm sure this hunk of yours hasn't any trouble getting it—"

"Lucy, please." Grace blushed and prayed Luke couldn't guess the drift of the conversation.

Lucy chortled. "I'll bet he's all over you. Heavy breathing? Wet kisses? Tearing at your clothing?"

"Not even close."

"Oh," Lucy said, disappointed. "Hmph. Does he have the same problem Kip had?"

"For heaven's sake!"

"Maybe he does," Lucy suggested. "After all, the ones who look like studs have a terribly difficult image to live up to. Perhaps he's terrible in bed because he's afraid of failing, and because he's afraid of failing, he's—"

"Good-bye, Lucy," Grace said curtly, cutting her off before she really got wound up. Lucy was the best kind of friend under almost every circumstance, but she had an impulsive imagination that usually ended up discomfiting Grace in one way or another. Grace continued, "I'll be in touch after I'm settled somewhere, all right? And I'll get to Cincinnati one way or another."

"Gray, don't you dare hang up before I ask—"

"Good-bye!" Grace gasped, and hung up hastily, feeling foolishly guilty with Luke the Laser himself sitting less than eighteen inches away. She knew she was breathing hard and tried to get a grip on herself once more.

Luke drove in silence for another half-mile as Grace fiddled nervously with her papers.

Finally, he asked, "Who's Kip? Your dog?"

CHAPTER FOUR

"YOU WEREN'T SUPPOSED to be listening," Grace snapped.

"Oh, so he's not a dog," Luke said, hearing her peeved tone. "Is he?"

"No."

Luke glanced across at her, but she looked away in time and they avoided each other's eyes. As if in challenge, he said, "He's your boyfriend, then. I see."

"No," Grace said firmly, "you don't see. I am certainly past the stage of having boyfriends, thank you. Kip is— was a good friend of mine, and we've parted company."

"And Lucy thinks...?" Luke prompted, ignoring her speech about boyfriends.

Without considering that she shouldn't say it, Grace replied to his question. "Frankly," she admitted uncomfortably, "Lucy believes I'm better off without Kip's company. Her opinion of him was never very high."

Luke smiled at that and nodded once. "I'm beginning to like Lucy even more."

Grace was at first annoyed by his response, but that

feeling didn't stick. Was Luke glad she didn't have a man in her life at the moment? Why would he be teasing her otherwise? She managed to catch herself before she smiled, and Luke was none the wiser.

She sneaked a look at him as he drove. Yes, Lucy would like Luke a lot, too. The animal type always attracted her most. The strange part was that Grace was finding *herself* attracted to Luke the Laser! There existed an unspoken magnetism between them, she decided. She felt drawn to him sexually, for crying out loud, and that had never happened to Grace Barrett before with such power. She was actually short of breath just from sitting next to him in his blasted car. His hand on the gearshift looked very large but not the least bit clumsy. She couldn't help wondering how he might use his long fingertips on her back or down the curve of her waist in a casual moment. And although he'd been in the shower just before they left Pittsburgh, he didn't smell perfumy like some men, just clean and nice. His hair was curly and might feel soft in her fingers.

Grace recognized the signs in herself. She wanted to experiment, to try touching him to see what reaction ignited in her own body. She wondered if her physical longing was as real as it felt. She was almost at the point of aching. She wanted to lay her hand along his arm or, better yet, on the solid length of his thigh, just to see what would happen.

The odd thing was that Luke either pretended the electricity between them wasn't there, or didn't feel like doing anything about it in spite of his casual verbal asides. That took her back a pace: Grace was baffled by his lack of interest. Was she really so undesirable? Or was Luke one of those men who preferred to befriend women with no sexual politics involved? Usually, Grace appreciated a man who could see her as a friend and not a bed partner. She enjoyed having male friends. But this was downright exasperating! Was she going to have to do something embarrassingly obvious to get his attention? Maybe Lucy was right. Maybe, like Kip, Luke wanted no intimate involvement with women. He certainly hadn't come close to making a pass. Why not?

She thought about it for another half hour in brooding silence. Luke was occupied with his own thoughts, and they shared the quiet without discomfort. In time, Luke turned on the radio and homed in on a heavy-metal rock-'n'-roll station. He kept the volume down, and hummed along with tunes Grace did not recognize.

"Do you have the station address handy?" Luke asked finally, interrupting her thoughts as he pulled the Jaguar onto an exit ramp of the highway. "We're almost into town."

Grace obeyed him and dug her notebook out of her attaché case. She read him the address. In just a few minutes, he was going to deliver her to the television station and she might never see him again. He was going to carry her luggage inside and say good-bye! If she was lucky, she might get a handshake. That thought set Grace into a stew. Realizing that she wanted to stay with him at least long enough to understand why he drew her attention so thoroughly, she decided that there had to be a way of prolonging their time together. She filed through the possibilities rapidly.

"Watch the street signs for me, will you?" Luke asked, interrupting her frantic thoughts.

So, trying to keep her eyes on the passing side streets and calling out the names and numbers, Grace decided she was going to have to do something desperate to keep Luke the Laser from heading back to Pittsburgh right away. She didn't know what yet, but she'd come up with something.

"How's the time?" Luke asked, when it looked as if they might be lost between side streets.

Grace checked her watch and was startled to find that it was after twelve-thirty. She had to be at the studio in less than half an hour for the one-thirty air time. Mocking herself with her underlying meaning, she said, "I'm not desperate yet."

"Yet," Luke repeated, amused by her tone of voice. He checked his side mirror and cut across the lane to make a left-hand turn.

The Jaguar accelerated smoothly, easing Grace back into her seat with a satisfying kind of power. She liked the feeling that the car controlled her at that moment, but wished that

Luke would take a little initiative, too. She didn't like being the aggressor, but he was forcing her into taking charge. If she didn't speak up, he was going to leave her. How was she going to manage it? By saying something corny? Something clever and sexy? Or maybe something *blunt* and sexy?

"Here we go," Luke said finally, and he drew the car to the curb. "I figured we'd find this place sooner or later. I hate to ask for directions."

"There must be some male hormone that prevents men from asking directions even if they're completely lost," Grace said, trying to sound lighthearted as she reached for her attaché case. "I've never known a man to stop at a gas station for help unless he can fake chitchat with the attendant while he fills the tank."

Luke set the parking brake and shut off the engine. He half turned to her. "I just don't like to admit I don't know where I'm going."

Grace laughed and found the handle of her bag. She pulled it into her lap. "Do you always know where you're going, Laser?"

A pause. Luke waited until Grace lifted her eyes and met his blue gaze directly, then he replied with a half-smile, "Always, Princess."

Grace swallowed hard. His eyes bore right into her head and made her mind go completely blank. So this was what it was like to think with one's hormones! Grace looked down to discover that she was clutching her attaché case for dear life, as if hugging it hard would suppress the sudden tripping and slamming of her heart. She said unevenly, "I see. Uh, well, I must hurry. Thank you very much. You've been very, very kind and I—It was above and beyond the call of gallantry to— I mean—"

"I enjoyed it," he said easily, reaching for his door handle, ready to get out of the car.

She had to stop him, no matter how humiliating it might seem later. Quickly, softly, Grace begged, "Luke!"

He turned back to her, half surprised, his hand still on the door handle.

"I'm being sincere," Grace stumbled ahead desperately.

"I never expected such generosity from you. I don't feel I can just say good-bye and leave."

When Luke didn't respond, she gave up trying to make sense and leaned impulsively toward him, careful to avoid bumping the brim of her hat. With discretion thrown to the winds, she gave Luke a brief show-biz kind of kiss on his cheek, a barest brushing of her lips against his freshly shaved face. Her nose touched the brown curl of his hair just above his ear, and that soft contact set her blood simmering. There! They merely had to touch, and Grace melted inside.

Luke might have sensed that involuntary melting, for she was so close that the front of her jacket rested on the bulky knit of his sweater. As if by instinct, he put his hand to the back of her head. He was gentle, though, just slipping his fingers through the tendrils of her hair at the nape of her neck. He held her there so that her cheek almost touched his for an instant.

Grace went still, her senses suddenly alert. He couldn't ignore her now! He didn't breathe, didn't speak, just hesitated, holding her head close to his. He smelled of wool and fresh winter air, along with the subtler and not unpleasant scent of automobiles. His hair brushed her temple and felt like the caress of autumn leaves in a noontime breeze. Grace closed her eyes to savor the rush of delightfully sudden sensations. Surely he could hear her heart go into a crazy patter of excitement?

Then Luke touched his nose to the delicate line of her jaw and took a long breath, as if inhaling the fragrance that might have clung to her there. It was slow and erotic, and Grace felt her reluctance dissolve entirely. In a moment, she might plead with him for a kiss.

But Luke didn't kiss her. In fact, an instant later he let her slide away, although he briefly trailed his fingertips along the sensitive flesh of her throat as he withdrew. His eyes were open and vivid, searching hers, and his mouth was pressed into a solemn straight line.

That solemnity brought Grace up short. Was he pretending to be serious? Or was he inwardly laughing at her foolish attempt to get his attention? His gaze was fairly sparkling with suppressed remarks, she could see. Stung, she began, "Well—"

But Luke popped open his door and said, "I'm not going to wrestle with you in here, Princess. Stay put."

Disconcerted, Grace remained in her seat while Luke maneuvered his long legs sideways and, with more than a little difficulty, got his big frame out of the low car. Although it was cold outside, he didn't reach for his jacket, but closed his door and strode around the front of the car with a loose-limbed but purposeful gait. Casting a single glance at the oncoming traffic—rather, Grace thought, like Moses commanding the Red Sea to part—Luke stepped up to her door and opened it. He reached down and drew her out into the sunshine. A horn blew in annoyance, but Luke didn't pay attention. Smoothly, he pulled her by the hand around the back of the car, moving so fast that Grace had to trot to keep up, her other hand clamped to her hat to keep it from being blown off. He stopped behind the car before they were even back on the sidewalk, and turned on Grace. He was very tall and suddenly full of authority. He took her hat between two fingers and, with a tweak, removed it from her head.

Grace lifted her chin, staring in surprise while the loose blond wisps of her hair blew around her upturned face. Now what? She was trembling with trepidation inside, and she knew her startled eyes were a dead giveaway. Had she let the evil genie out of the bottle?

Simply, Luke said, "I don't want to muss you up before your show, but—"

He pulled her hand to his hip and let her go so that she had to touch him there or drop her hand completely. His own hand traveled swiftly up her arm and shoulder until he found the nape of her neck again. Neatly, he pulled her slender body into his solid frame. Then he tipped her face higher and sought her eyes with his. He *was* laughing inside this time, Grace was sure. The sparkle in his blue gaze couldn't be caused by the blaze of winter sunshine.

"To hell with that lovely lipstick of yours," he said. "Kiss me, Princess."

On a crowded street in the middle of the day with half of Cleveland on its lunch hour, watching! Grace Barrett, etiquette columnist for some of the biggest newspapers in the country! She closed her eyes instinctively and lifted her mouth to meet the lips of one Luke "the Laser" Lazurnovich, ex–wide receiver for the Pittsburgh Steelers. Madness! Tacky, gauche, unspeakably inappropriate madness! At the last second, she almost remembered herself and protested, "Luke—"

His mouth smothered the word, taking her lips so swiftly that she didn't have time to draw a breath. It wasn't a gentle kiss but a hurried one that rushed too quickly into the exploratory stage. His lips were firm though not hard, teasing though not hurting. He tasted warm and good, and with an easy nudge, he parted her mouth with his, taking a bold liberty before she even dreamed of granting him the privilege. Then he tilted her head to one side with the leverage of his body, making his next wish clear. He wanted to taste her mouth, to learn its contour and texture in a very short time. He slanted his mouth across hers, but gyrated her head until the contact was perfect once more. His tongue was quick, licking skillfully once across the line of her lower lip until she yielded and let him enter. He tasted her then, and rolled her tongue with his in an erotic maneuver that taunted the last vestiges of her sense of propriety.

With her own tongue burning under his insistent exploration, Grace felt a hot wave of liquid desire surge up from within herself with the speed of tumultuous floodwaters. From her thighs to the very spot where her breasts were squeezed against Luke's hard chest, she was on fire. It was delicious, and she weakly leaned into his powerful body until they were locked in an embrace of undeniable passion. Without thinking, she tightened her hand on the curve of his hip, testing the hard contour of muscle there. With just a swift, slipping motion, she could grasp his behind, if she wanted to. But playing it safer and with the attaché case in one hand, Grace lifted her other hand to touch his side where the curve of his lean waist met the hardness of his lower rib cage. Even through the sweater, she could feel the won-

derful strength in his frame, the tensile beauty of his body.
He felt hard yet tempered, and very warm. Grace clung to
him, seeking his heat against the cold air around them.

Enough. His body communicated the word half a minute
later. The kiss had been breathless and fast and stupefying,
but now it was over. His mouth clung gently while he
loosened his hold on the nape of her neck. He released her
mouth and her neck, but took the last instant to touch his
lips one final time against the pulsing length of her exposed
throat. Grace heard her own breath suck in as if she'd been
drowned in sensual pleasures, and she plummeted back into
reality. She let Luke go and stepped backward in confusion.

But he swiftly grabbed her wrist and hauled her toward
him once more. Another horn blared from the street, and
Grace jumped at the sound. In her desire-induced trance,
she'd barely missed getting run over! Luke was laughing,
and he pulled her up onto the sidewalk with the air of a
bemused parent leading a docile child.

"There," he said, when they had gained the safe side of
the car. He turned to her once more. "I'm the wrong size
for adolescent wrestling matches in cars. Good luck with
your show, all right?"

"Luke—" Grace said stupidly, blushing like a kid. How
embarrassing! On the street! How many times had she chided
readers about flaunting their amorous tendencies in public?
To fall apart like a long-denied nymphomaniac was even
worse! She was walking like a newborn colt, her legs hardly
stable enough to support her weight. Luke had thoroughly
demolished her cool in the space of half a minute!

"Run along," he said.

"But—"

"Go on," he encouraged blandly. "I'll apologize later.
I'll be here when you finish."

She didn't have time to question or argue, and she wasn't
sure she could put three words together and make them
sound sensible. With her poise destroyed, she took a tot-
tering step away from him, and then another. The sidewalk
was busy, but the lunch-hour crowd made a path around the
two of them. That crowd! How many had seen Grace Barrett

in a primitive clinch? Her cheeks were burning, but it was too late now. She wheeled around and found that Luke was still watching. He didn't look the least bit sorry for having embarrassed her. In fact, he was looking decidedly pleased with himself. He twirled her hat on the end of his forefinger and smiled at her with lazy-lidded assurance.

Grace summoned her self-control and opened her attaché case. Stepping back to Luke, she withdrew the copy of *Ms. Barrett's Etiquette for Every Occasion* she had intended to give to the talk-show host who was about to interview her. Instead, she slapped the book onto Luke's chest and said firmly, "Chapter Eight, Laser."

He grabbed the book to keep it from falling, relinquished her hat, and said nothing. His grin was enough. He knew exactly what he'd done to her composure.

Grace executed an about-face and marched to the television station hoping that she wasn't going to slip on the ice or stumble over a crack in the pavement or further humiliate herself with Luke watching.

Dear Ms. Barrett,

A gentleman friend of mine insists on making public displays of affection that cause me great embarrassment. I've discussed my feelings with him, but he hasn't gotten the point yet. I'm ready for drastic measures. What can I do?

—In a Quandry in Quebec

Dear Bec,

You have two choices, of course. If you're more embarrassed than in love, dump him. If you'd rather eat peas with a knife than live without the man, then use every skill and weapon you've got to teach him some manners. I believe in positive reinforcement. Many parents give their children a treat for behaving correctly. The question is, what might your gentleman consider a treat?

CHAPTER FIVE

EVEN WITH HALF her mind in a holding pattern, Grace managed to summon her Barrett poise and articulation during her television interview. She fielded questions from the studio audience with the wryly witty responses that were her trademark, and then led the host through the rituals of an afternoon tea. She poured from a silver teapot and was her most gracious self when the host spilled fake watercress sandwiches down her trouser leg. The program went well from a public-relations standpoint. Lucy would be pleased.

It was after three o'clock when Grace disengaged herself from the station staff. She refused their offers for a cab to a prominent hotel, crossing her fingers behind her back for good luck. And when she went through the double glass door and to the sidewalk outside, Providence was with her. There was Luke, standing precisely where she'd left him.

He'd put on his jacket, though, and a set of headphones was resting on his collarbones like a necklace. He'd been listening to music, obviously, but now he was talking cheerfully with a uniformed policeman under a steady fall of Christmaslike snow. Grace didn't think twice about the policeman until he tore a ticket out of his little black notebook and handed it over to Luke, who accepted it politely and turned to Grace with a pleasant smile. "Hullo. How'd it go?"

"Fine," she said, looking after the cop even as Luke took her elbow in hand to lead her to the car. "Have you been here all this time?"

"No. I made that delivery I told you about, and had some lunch." Luke stuck the ticket in his breast pocket, then pulled her to the Jaguar, where he had a large road map spread open on the roof and weighted down with a half-empty jar of dry-roasted peanuts. He handed the jar to Grace. "Are you hungry?"

"A little, yes," she admitted, taking the peanuts out of reflex. She was not going to lower herself to eating on the street, however. It wouldn't do to stoop to Luke's level of behavior, not if she was going to teach him a thing or two. She looked at his map. "What are you doing?"

Luke held down the corner of the map against the still-brisk breeze. He pulled Grace closer until her body was sheltered by his and he could look over her shoulder at the map. "See?" His voice was gentle at her ear, causing the flesh along her arms to break out in goosebumps. How could a man sound so sexy with a single word? He continued, "I figure we can make Cincinnati by eight o'clock. We shoot down this highway and head west. Easy."

Grace blinked at the map, conscious that his chest and her shoulders were fitted together like the pieces of a jigsaw puzzle. Not only that, but the rounded curve of her own bottom had automatically sought the snug heat of his loins against the dropping temperature and snow. The sunshine was gone, and winter had returned. Grace remained hunched against Luke's body, although her brain screamed that she should not.

"An easy drive, if the weather holds," he went on, drawing their proposed route with his fingertip to show her. "In my opinion, there's not a decent place to stay in this town, and Cincinnati's got a hotel that will knock even *your* socks off. What d'you say?"

Grace kept her back to him and asked flatly, "Luke, did you read Chapter Eight of my book?"

He let go of the map and caught it neatly in one hand. He stood back and began to fold it up again. "Nope."

Grace turned and looked at him hard, her eyes narrowed and stern. "I asked you to read it."

With his eyes twinkling from under their heavy lids, he corrected, "Not very politely, I might add. Look, Princess, haven't you ever heard about old dogs and new tricks? Hell, the very title of that chapter was enough to turn me off."

"'Courtship Rituals of the American Male'? What's wrong with that? It was supposed to be funny."

Luke pretended to shudder as he pulled his headphones from around his neck and began to wind up the thin cord. "I'll admit I fit the American male part, but, Princess, is this a courtship?"

Flushing, Grace snapped, "I realize that running off to a hotel in Cincinnati might mean one thing to a man of your background, but to me—"

"Easy, easy," he soothed, shoving the map and the headphones into his jacket pocket. "I haven't tried to jump your bones yet, have I?"

Appalled, Grace jerked her head up and squeaked, "Jump my—!"

"Relax. Take it easy. This is a no-pressure situation, okay? I'm taking a few days off, that's all, and we just so happen to be heading in the same direction."

"Look, Laser," Grace began, agitated by how quickly their conversation had deteriorated into disagreeable vulgarities, "you've got to understand that I am not the kind of woman who sleeps with men she barely knows. If you have some kind of erotic fantasy playing in the back of your mind, you may as well turn that pretty car of yours around and—"

"Hey," he said softly, stopping her. His face looked comically hurt, as if her suspicions had wounded him deeply.

With innocently rounded eyes and uplifted palms, he protested, "Have I once made an improper suggestion? I admit I lost my head when I kissed you, but that was just supposed to be for good luck. Can I help it if you suddenly turned into the warmest thing since hot buttered rum and—"

"I did no such thing!" Grace objected, affronted. "I was startled. I did *not* encourage you! I am *not* accustomed to being attacked on the street unless by a purse snatcher, so don't expect me to take that particular scene with good grace!"

"Then we're fighting about nothing," Luke said. "Right? I didn't mean to kiss you, and you didn't mean to kiss me. It was an accident. We'll call a truce, all right? If we can agree to keep our hands off each other, why can't we drive down to Cincinnati together?"

"I will certainly keep my hands off you!" Grace exclaimed in a blaze of outrage. "What a suggestion!"

Looking amused and unconvinced, Luke nodded, eyeing her askance. "Uh-huh."

"For heaven's sake!" Grace blushed in spite of her resolve to play the part of shocked Victorian lady. She hadn't expected Luke to take this course at all, and she was certainly not about to admit her feelings to him now. He actually believed that she was—as Lucy might say in one of her more crude moments—warm for his form. She demanded, "What do you take me for?"

Luke took her elbow placidly and began to lead her around the front of the car again. "What do I take you for, Princess? A woman, that's all. An attractive one, I admit, but fortunately one who isn't demanding that I drop my pants and try setting some records for Masters and Johnson."

That did it. Grace felt her face turn hot with humiliation. Had he guessed her motives for that innocent peck on the cheek in his car? Had he suspected that she had got from him exactly what she'd been hoping for? A sizzling kiss had been just what she planned, no matter what she was telling him now. With her voice rising too high and becoming very sharp, she sputtered, "I am not—repeat *not*—interested in sex! Least of all, with—with the likes of you!"

"Good. Look, this is a comfortable kind of something we've got here. If we agree to stay out of the bedroom, it's kind of nice, don't you think?"

"We are completely different kinds of people," she objected firmly.

"Right," Luke agreed, opening the car door for her. "Think of it as a cultural exchange."

"Oh, heavens!"

"Ready? Cincinnati, Princess?"

He guided her down into the car and she slid into the seat before she could catch her breath. He closed the door after her. From her half-reclining position in the low sports car, she watched him round the front of the car. Had he been serious? Had that kiss been merely for good luck? Was she back at square one? Didn't Luke see that she was a woman with a core like caramel?

Dear Ms. Barrett,

In a weak moment, I recently agreed to a disagreeable suggestion that the man of my dreams has been proposing for some time. I'm having second thoughts now and would like to know how to rescind my acceptance and forgo his suggested romantic tryst in the country. How shall I save face and my virtue without sending Mr. Wonderful off to admire my sisters?

—Too Many Sisters in Tucson

Dear Tu,

It sounds as though you're having second thoughts about your second thoughts. For your first choice, you can conveniently come down with a case of the flu just before the appointed weekend. For your second choice, I propose that you honestly confront the gentleman and tearfully explain your misgivings. Done properly, this tactic often produces the best results. Your third option is to go and have a good time with the man of your dreams and the devil with your sisters,

*but Ms. Barrett would never dream of suggesting such
a thing.*

Grace decided that no matter what, she was going to find
out if Luke the Laser was a man or a monk. She would
indeed allow him to take her to Cincinnati. Her fear of flying
had nothing to do with the decision. She wanted to stay
with him a little longer, that was all. The man was positively
irresistible in a crude kind of way.

And she was interested in a hotel that, in Luke's words,
would "knock her socks off." What did a professional football player consider a nice hotel? One that provided an
unceasing supply of beer in cans so that one might rip off
the aluminum tops and quaff the brew from around the sharp
metal edges? And in Cincinnati, for heaven's sake? It was
bound to be an interesting trip, no matter what.

So Grace sat back in the leather seat and popped a few
peanuts to keep her hunger pangs at bay. She let Luke find
the right road for Cincinnati, Ohio.

It turned out that he had seen her interview on the talk
show after all. He'd had lunch at a bar in a suburb called
Shaker Heights, not far from where he'd made his delivery,
and he'd seen the program there. Grace found herself laughing with Luke about the show. He had gotten a big charge
out of the host dropping the plate of sandwiches and Grace's
tranquil barb that had heightened the comedy of the moment.
To continue the smooth flow of conversation, she had observed sweetly, "Oh, I see you must have played football
in high school. A wide receiver, were you?" Her joke had
been for Luke's benefit, and he knew it.

Then Grace asked Luke about his business and learned
that he was not a car dealer, as she'd first thought, but a
restorer of classic automobiles, mostly fine old Jaguars. He
did little of the real work himself, of course, but owned the
garage and dabbled with cars that interested him. He also
supplied parts to Jaguar fanciers who were unable to locate
what they needed to restore their own cars. He had paid just
such a visit to a fellow Jaguar-lover that afternoon, a retired

physician, he said, who was refitting a coupe that Luke admired very much.

In talking with him, Grace decided that Luke was probably financially secure, although he didn't display many signs of great wealth. Surely he had made a bundle playing professional football, and with luck he might have invested it wisely. Now he apparently lived modestly, enjoying small pleasures, she suspected. He didn't object to an occasional extravagance, however. He took yearly trips to England to obtain a supply of parts for his beloved cars, and he apparently liked to travel once he was abroad. In conversation, he mentioned a car he had seen in Germany, so Grace supposed he was well traveled, perhaps more so than she was herself. She found herself wondering if he traveled alone.

The conversation turned to places they had both visited, and finally they compared notes about London. That conversation quickly highlighted the differences in their tastes, for Grace preferred the intimate Cadogan, a dignified old hotel near Sloane Street that provided tea and scones and very attentive room service. Luke liked the horse races and the pubs and the soccer games, where everyone sang the "Hallelujah Chorus" after each goal. They talked naturally about their differences, however, and Grace was oddly pleased by that.

By eight o'clock Grace was tired and hungry and getting drowsy, so Luke turned up the volume on the radio and roared along the last highway into Cincinnati. He found the hotel easily.

Grace was astonished. The Omni Netherland Plaza was a grand hotel, a masterpiece of art deco magnificence straight out of a Fred Astaire movie. How such a spectacular place ended up in a small and unassuming Ohio town, she couldn't imagine. It reminded her of photographs she had seen of the gracious old ocean liners, with their luxury and style elevated to an art form.

Luke left his precious car with a bowing attendant and took Grace up the marble stairs to the streamlined lobby, where a pair of desk clerks greeted them with dignity and pleasure. While Luke saw to the details of registering, Grace looked around in frank amazement. Although her knowledge of interior design and architecture could sustain her only during a casual cocktail-party conversation, she recognized the unique beauty of the restored hotel. She noticed a Babylonian unicorn in a lovely fountain, rococo ceiling murals, and beautifully dainty wrought-iron railings that looked like finely carved French Quarter grilles. Gilt, brass, rosewood, and marble were used lavishly to decorate and enhance exquisitely simple lines. The whole building exuded an ambience of grandeur and elegance rarely seen in modern times.

Luke was smiling to himself when Grace turned on him in delight.

"This is amazing!" she cried softly, taking his arm out of instinct. "How did you know about this place?"

Luke shrugged it off. "Stick with me, Princess. I know all the towns that have a team in the AFC."

"AFC?" Grace asked cautiously as they started up the carpeted grand staircase beneath a gloriously brilliant chandelier.

"Forget I mentioned it," he said with a laugh, shaking his head.

"You called this a cultural exchange," Grace protested immediately. "Come on, Laser, start explaining. What's an AFC?"

"American Football Conference," Luke said, giving up. He helped Grace into the elevator and followed her in.

The bellhop joined them, and in a silence of anticipation they rode upward. Grace felt her spirits rise with that elevator. She was excited, she realized. She should probably be nervous about what to expect. Perhaps Luke had booked them into the same room—into the same bathroom and the same bed. But she wasn't nervous. Not really. She was learning to trust Luke, blast him. He wasn't going to "jump her bones," she knew. He was a safe date. Unfortunately.

What awaited them on the other side of the elevator doors was an exquisite suite of rooms unrivaled by any Grace had

ever seen in fine European hotels. She took a painful breath
of astonishment when she stepped through the foyer and
into the sitting room.

Awed, she glanced around at the highly stylized chintz
chairs; elegant ornamental tables; lavish curtains, which
heightened the drama of a drapery motif in the architectural
appointments; a lovely, lush carpet; and dusky light from
frosted lamps in the the classic art-deco style. The rooms
were fantasy-wonderful and reminiscent of the twenties in
Paris. The bellhop briefly disappeared with their luggage,
then returned to switch on lamps, fluff the bouquet of fragrant orchids in a froth of ferns, and adjust the sweeping
curtains at the terrace doors so that the lights of Cincinnati
glowed beyond the tall windows.

While Luke tipped the bellhop and discussed the work-
ings of the fireplace, Grace crossed to the French doors.
She lifted the latch and went outside into the night air. A
secluded terrace wound around potted evergreen trees, and
although the flower boxes were full of snow and the tracks
of winter wrens, Grace could easily imagine them full of
riotous red geraniums and striped fronds. Unmindful of the
cold, she went to the intricately designed railing and looked
out into the night sky. Her heart was beating with delight.
She had never expected such pleasant surroundings, and she
needed some time to absorb it all.

Luke joined her a few minutes later. He had left his
jacket indoors and came strolling out with his hands thrust
into the front pockets of his jeans. He glanced around,
getting his bearings, then went over to Grace.

She turned and leaned against the railing, hugging her
elbows against the cold and lifting her face to smile at him.
"This is wonderful!"

"I told you it would be. I'm full of surprises."

Grace's smile was wry with understanding through the
half-light. "I'll remember that."

He shook his head. "Truce, remember? It's freezing out
here, and there's a fire inside. Come in."

Grace didn't take his arm, even though she was tempted
to, but she sauntered at his side toward the doors. She had

to start figuring him out, so she remarked, "You're easily made hungry or cold, I'm discovering. You're a man who wants his needs met immediately, I think."

"Usually," Luke agreed languidly, and he then paused. "Look."

Grace followed his gaze and saw the warm sitting room glowing by the light of the frosted lamps and the flicker of firelight in the marble hearth. The elegant furniture, its delicate mauve fabric glimmering with reflected light, looked inviting and romantic, as if simply waiting for a couple to come in and enjoy the quiet seclusion.

Grace sighed at the sight. In spite of the pretty room, she shivered under a fresh blast of winter air. Luke moved behind her at once and pulled her against his body to keep her warm. His arms closed in front of her, his hands lying flat across her belly. In her ear, he murmured, "You figured I'd take you to a motel with mirrors on the ceiling and hourly rates, I'll bet. Maybe an X-rated movie and a six-pack of beer for kicks?"

Grace chuckled, snuggling closer—for warmth, she assured herself, and not to enjoy the soft tickle of his lips against her sensitive earlobe. She might scare him off if she responded to him now, so she nodded and added with a low laugh, "With a tiger-striped bedspread and a neon sign out front."

Luke rocked her playfully backward, sealing the last centimeter between their bodies. "Disappointed?"

"Not yet," Grace retorted lightly. "We haven't checked the bedrooms for animal skins yet. And maybe there are dirty movies on the television."

"I doubt it. I'd have remembered that, I'm sure."

Grace twisted out of his embrace then and asked in surprise, "You mean you've really stayed here before? At this hotel?"

"Not this particular suite," Luke said, catching her hand and leading her back into the warmth and light of their rooms. "But sure, I've stayed here. It's against the law to discriminate, y'know. Besides, only football teams can afford these prices on a regular basis. Are you hungry?"

Sorry that she'd been so obvious in her surprise, Grace admitted quickly, "Yes. Hungrier than the Pittsburgh Steelers could ever have been. Let me look around the suite before we go downstairs, though. I'd like to explore up here. Luke, this is really special."

Grace could see that he was pleased by her reaction to his choice of accommodations. He followed her slowly as she opened this door and that, uncovering the spectacular bathroom with its luxurious tub and sterling silver fixtures. Then the first bedroom with an elevated double bed and shafts of soft light that showed the draped side curtains in theatrical splendor. Luke's duffel bag had been laid neatly across the luggage rack. In the doorway of the second room, Luke leaned his shoulder against the doorjamb while Grace oohed and aahed over the bed's watered silk coverlet and the satin pillows on a dusty-rose divan. Her feet were soundless on the plush white carpet.

She sat down gingerly at the vanity table. In the mirror, she saw her face softly illuminated by the wall-mounted lamps and the wisps of her loosened hair catching golden light from those same lamps. Even in her tailored jacket, she looked ethereal and feminine. It must have been the magic of the romantic setting that brought such pretty color to her cheekbones. Her reflection caught Grace unawares, and she looked into her own startled gray-blue eyes for a split second.

From the doorway, Luke spoke up again, sounding oddly hoarse. "We could have dinner sent up, if you like."

"Oh, no," Grace said right away, glancing over her shoulder at his relaxed stance. "I'd love to see the rest of the hotel."

With another peek at her reflection in the mirror, she realized that her hair was actually tumbled and unkempt and that her eye shadow had begun to crease. Suddenly, she didn't want Luke to see her in such a state, even if the lights and soft pink surroundings had lent a special glow to her appearance. Her lipstick was long gone, so she glanced around for her luggage, ready to repair her makeup. "Just give me a minute to freshen up, and I'll be ready to go," she told Luke.

He shrugged and left the room abruptly, saying from out in the hallway. "Suit yourself, Princess."

He walked away, and Grace wondered thoughtfully for a moment. Perhaps *he*'d rather use room service than accompany her to a civilized public restaurant. Almost everyone Grace knew was uncomfortable displaying their table manners for Ms. Barrett, and Luke was probably no different. He was undoubtedly terrified of showing his uncouth manners to her with an audience on hand.

Oh, well, this was as good a time as any to start her campaign to polish Luke's etiquette. Keeping Eliza Doolittle, Shaw's flower seller-*cum*-socialite, in mind, Ms. Barrett was going to teach Luke the Laser that gracious living was better than dripping sandwiches in front of the home fireplace. She'd charm him into feeling comfortable and gradually show him the right way to act. He'd never even know he was getting a lesson.

The best way to get him feeling good about himself was to win his confidence and boost his ego. Perhaps Lucy was right. Perhaps women expected too much of Luke the Laser and blew his confidence. He'd said himself that he was thankful Grace hadn't pressured him into proving his manhood. If she flirted with him in a low-key way to bolster his self-confidence, she was probably safe. Luke wasn't dying to jump into bed with her, and Grace certainly had no intentions of forcing him. Or so she told herself. She'd learned with Kip that lovemaking suggested by the woman was the surest way to an exasperating bout of impotence. For a while, there had been a happy medium with Kip—no talk of sex, but only the subtle suggestion that any overtures toward intimacy he might make wouldn't be rejected. That was probably the answer with Luke, too. This careful carrot dangled in front of his nose might make him eager to learn the art of civilized behavior.

Grace let down her hair and combed it smooth. Then she reapplied her makeup and hung her jacket in the wardrobe. Still dressed in her ruffled red blouse and white wool trousers, she went out to meet Luke looking elegant and cool.

He had stripped off his sweater and was standing in front

of an arched, gilded mirror near the fireplace in his jeans and shirt. He had just threaded a knit tie through the collar of his powder-blue shirt, but at the sight of Grace coming out of the bedroom, he clumsily bungled the knot.

"Here," she said, crossing to help him. Standing before him with the two ends of his tie in her hands, she smiled and said, "I'm a fussbudget for straight ties. Shall I?"

Luke stood very still, chin up, while she arranged the knot again. He cleared his throat uncomfortably. "Uh, Princess, I've been thinking. About this, I mean. You and me tonight."

"So have I," Grace said calmly, slipping the end of the tie through the knot. "Are you having second thoughts?"

"A few," Luke admitted with care. "Do you know what you've gotten yourself into, Princess Grace? With me? A guy with very little sophistication when it comes to these things?"

So he *was* worried about his restaurant manners, poor dear. Grace wriggled the knot up into his collar and said softly, "Believe me, Luke, nothing you do is going to shock me. I've had a great deal of experience. I'm an expert, and I should know. You've got more going for you than you realize."

Luke watched her then with a puzzled shadow in his eyes and a hint of a smile on his mouth. "Do you really think so?"

"Of course," Grace said, giving his tie a final pat. She left her hand there, resting on his chest. She could feel his breathing become ragged under her touch. He must be nervous, she thought. She smiled up into his eyes and said, "There. I'm ready when you are."

"Really?" Luke asked, slipping his hands around her waist. With deliciously inexorable strength, he drew her body close until her belly ground provocatively against his. Coming close to kiss her, he promptly demonstrated that she had miscalculated terribly. Before his lips began their descent, he murmured, "I thought you wanted dinner first."

CHAPTER SIX

LUKE BENT HIS head little by little, and Grace's own mouth lifted as if by magic to meet his until their breaths seemed to touch. Then Grace remembered all the peanuts she'd just eaten and how her lips were going to taste, and with that stupid thought, cold, clear reality knifed through her fogged brain in time to prevent the kiss from happening. Hold it. Did he mean that he felt desire for her now? She froze in his embrace and pressed her left hand hard against his chest. Holding him off thus, she stared up into his eyes. "Wh-what did you say?"

Seeing the startled expression on her face, he relaxed his grip on her right away. With his right hand, though, he cupped the soft curve of her upper arm, holding her effortlessly near. The heat of his thigh practically burned through the layers of fabric to Grace's own, but she didn't draw away from that magnetic warmth. Luke must have felt that contact acutely, too, for he remained motionless, but with a grin on his mouth and his eyes half closed. "Forgive

me. I lost my head for a second. I had an incredible urge
to kiss you again, but I caught it in time."

Bewildered, Grace began, "I thought you—that you didn't
want—couldn't—"

"I didn't want what?"

"Me," Grace blurted out foolishly. "I thought you had
a problem."

"A problem," Luke repeated, eyeing her cautiously but
with his smile undimmed. "What kind of problem?"

Grace couldn't stop herself. She was staring up into his
flickering blue gaze like a starry-eyed idol worshiper, feeling the heat of his beautifully huge body and trembling with
the knowledge that he had been about to kiss her. She heard
her own voice say, "With women. I—you never indicated
any interest, and you kept dropping remarks. About women
making the first move and inhibiting your—your performance. How you appreciated that I didn't expect you to
drop your trousers and—Oh, dear, I assumed that you were—
were—"

"Oh," Luke interrupted, comprehending finally. *"That*
problem. I see."

"It's not uncommon," Grace said quickly. "It's nothing
to be ashamed of, of course. I didn't mean to imply that
you *had* to be interested in me, but I wondered at first, and
then—"

"Well," Luke interrupted again, dropping his eyes away
from hers and loosening her arm imperceptibly, "it's not a
subject that I enjoy talking about, y'know."

Grace swiftly touched his chest, laying both hands there
to soothe him. She stepped against him then until her breasts
rested lightly against his chest and her thighs melted gently
into his. "I understand," she said, matching the intimacy of
his hesitant voice. "Don't let it bother you, all right? I didn't
mean to open any wounds."

Automatically, Luke lifted his hands to her back and
caressed her there, as if absently. He couldn't meet her
eyes, but his face was carefully set in an excruciatingly
serious expression. His voice taut, he said, "I'm sure I'll

be all right. Just please don't expect too much from me, Princess."

"No, I won't," Grace promised.

And then, only to comfort him of course, she stood on tiptoe and pressed a gentle, sisterly kiss to his cheek.

Luke's hand slid easily upward until he had captured the nape of her neck in the cup of his palm. He held her head, tipping her face up to his until he could see her eyes. At the same time, his other arm wound smoothly around her body until he had locked her to his frame in a shy but nevertheless sexual embrace. His fingers played into her hair. "Princess," he murmured gratefully, with such softness that Grace had to strain closer to hear, "you're making me feel a way I haven't felt in a very long time."

Any woman's nurturing instincts would have been aroused the way Grace's were. He needed her help. And she wouldn't dream of refusing this poor, unfortunate young man. Look what the rest of heartless womankind had inflicted on him! A virile, attractive man cut down in the prime of his sexually active life! And he needed *her!* Not Bo Derek or Sophia Loren or any other female sex symbol, but her, Grace Barrett. Luke was cautiously, uneasily, hesitantly, asking for her tender help.

If he only knew the kinds of carnal thoughts that were suddenly seething in her brain, she thought, Luke would surely drop her like the proverbial hot potato and run for safety. She mustn't let him see that he was turning her bones to quivering jelly. She had to compliment him now and build his shaken confidence without unnerving him at the crucial moment. Remaining outwardly calm, she managed a small smile and murmured, "You're doing the same to me."

Luke smiled, slowly drawing her upward. In a singsong whisper against her lips, he said, "Nooo kidding?"

And then he kissed her, drawing her that last half centimeter to himself until their mouths met and clung with delicious tranquillity. Luke's firm lips were parted from the start, urging Grace's to match and meld. His tongue was there, too, brushing hers provocatively before the kiss grew in fervor. Grace felt her blood surge, pounding suddenly in her lips where their heartbeats pulsed together, racing to seek a common tempo.

Luke tilted her head and deepened the contact. He dipped swiftly, urgently, farther into the secluded cavern of Grace's mouth. He seemed to be making a more than physical exploration, Grace thought dimly; it was as though while experimenting with her lips he was judging her thoughts by the small, involuntary responses she gave. She tried to subdue the prompt surge of desire in herself but heard her breath suck in at once the moment he tightened his arm and forced her to slide her arms around his neck. Beneath her silk blouse, she felt her nipples contract with delight, and her stomach quivered with the shock and ripple of excited tension. He dragged her hard against him so she could feel and absorb the contours of his honed body with her own. His hand drifted blindly down her back, his fingers kneading at her flesh until he met the softer, rounder curve beneath her trousers, and then with strength, he molded her there, pressing, lifting her pelvis until she fit against him intimately.

The suggestion, the question, the request for more perhaps, was clear yet fleeting. Luke went no further. As if remembering his problem, he relaxed abruptly and let her go. Unconsciously, Grace made sure the last parts of them to separate were their lips.

Luke drew a safe distance away from her, looking surprised. Whether it was at himself or at her, Grace couldn't be sure.

She put her fingertips to her mouth, wondering if her sensitive flesh there looked as scorched as it felt. Her eyes were wide and turbulent.

"Well," Luke said, holding her gaze with his and allowing the smallest of smiles. "I may be on the road to recovery."

Grace let out an uneven breath, for her insides were still in a turmoil of awakened passion. What a kiss! For a man who was concerned for his performance in bed, he was pretty terrific in a clinch! With her own confidence shaken a bit, Grace whispered, "Let's not press our luck, all right?"

Luke laughed suddenly and turned away from her. Grace stood awkwardly by the fireplace, catching her balance on the mantel while he gathered up his Harris Tweed jacket and began to shrug into it. He said lightly, "To tell the truth, I'm too weak from hunger to try anything else right now."

Grace cleared her throat and rallied her composure. It was silly to act like a teenager who'd just been kissed for the first time. "So am I," she said.

"No kidding? I'd never guess." Luke fell back easily into the guise of the big dumb lug out on the town. He dropped his sophistication like a fumbled football and asked bluntly, "Doesn't your stomach make any noise when it's empty, or does blue blood prevent that phenomenon?"

Just at the time she had begun to believe he was a desirable man, he had to go and act like a dopey football player! Grace was embarrassed for having acted so impulsively. What a fool she could be! She was feeling like a Florence Nightingale, saving poor helpless Luke from the perils of impotence! Why was that role so appealing, for heaven's sake? While Luke led the way to the door and pulled it open for her, she said with a trace of her old asperity, "The solution is never to allow one's stomach to become so empty that passersby can hear it complaining."

"Oh, I remember," Luke countered, following her into the hall. "You finished all the peanuts in the car. No wonder you're so smug right now. This way."

With her dignity smarting, Grace rode the elevator with him, and they found their way to the Palm Court restaurant.

Graced by the prancing unicorn fountain and a spectacular drapery motif, the intimately illuminated room had a theatrical Egyptian flare that was breathtaking. The sloe-eyed hostess came swishing up from between the tables in a black cocktail dress and pearls. She appeared startled to find a man of Luke's size awaiting her services. Never glancing at Grace, she looked him up and down with dark brown eyes that practically turned to molasses as she absorbed his appearance. Grace wouldn't have been surprised to see the woman lick her lips before speaking to him.

"Can I help you, sir?"

Luke requested a table and held up two fingers to indicate how many chairs they required. It was a good thing he did that, Grace thought as she followed the hostess across the rose and celery carpet to a quiet banquette, for the other woman's mind obviously had gone blank in the face of such masculine perfection. The hostess was so agog that she only left one menu at the table.

So they shared the menu, and Grace overcame her annoyance with the hostess. She found herself exclaiming in delight over the listed entrées, and quickly found herself in the dilemma of choosing either the poached salmon in a sorrel sauce or truffled *coquilles*, both of which were her favorite dishes. The menu was largely in French, which Grace easily handled. If Luke had any problems with the language, he wasn't going to admit it. He ordered the salmon after Grace selected the scallops, and then he suggested that she choose a wine that she liked. On the proffered list, she found a Moselle that she remembered from a summer weekend in Tuxedo Park. Luke ordered it, and the waiter departed.

A small vase stood in the middle of the table, containing three velvety red tulips and a sprig of baby's breath. Grace touched the delicate petals with her fingertips. "Aren't they lovely?"

Pragmatically, Luke asked, "Where'd anybody get tulips this time of year?"

"They're nice," Grace declared, feeling happy. "They make me think of spring and new beginnings."

Luke smiled, for he had been watching Grace's eyes as they softened and warmed on the flowers. When the wine came and they were left alone again, he lifted his glass and solemnly made a toast. "I was going to drink to snowstorms, but let's toast tulips instead, all right?"

Laughing, Grace drank also. Luke held her eyes as the wine slipped down her throat, communicating his pleasure at finding himself alone with her. She decided that Luke could sometimes be a real smoothie, with the elements of seduction clearly enumerated in his head, perhaps even with illustrations. She had a fleeting feeling that he was miles ahead of her just now. If she hadn't known to the contrary, Grace would have supposed that Luke was as far from sexual dysfunction as Casanova. She brushed the thought aside.

It didn't take long before they were conversing again with the same kind of cameraderie they had enjoyed in the car that afternoon. Cautiously, they began to find out about each other's life.

"Have you always worked for your mother?" Luke asked when the soup had come.

"Oh, no," Grace said easily, picking up the correct spoon and noting that Luke waited until she had made the right choice before he followed suit. She dipped into the soup bowl and explained, "I worked as a copy editor for a publishing house for a few years after college and became Mother's secretary just three years ago after her old faithful left."

"Left? You mean retired?"

"No, she quit," Grace replied. She might as well tell all to Luke, she decided. He wasn't likely to sell revelations of the Barrett's dirty laundry to the sleazy tabloids. She tipped her head, as if imparting global secrets, and confided, "Mother is impossibly difficult to work for. She bullied, insulted, and terrorized Miss DeMillet daily. Finally, Mother threw an éclair at her, and the old girl up and quit."

"An éclair?" Luke echoed, crowing with laughter, unmindful of the other restaurant patrons nearby. "Is that the proper food to throw at employees? I thought a cream pie was the accepted weapon."

"No, no," Grace said, joining in the jest. "Éclairs are in much better taste. How's that for a pun? Although Mother is believed to be the epitome of good breeding, she has her fishwife side now and then. Fortunately, the public has never gotten wind of it."

Luke caught himself blowing across his soup and hastily put the spoon back in the bowl. "So you took over for Miss DeMillet?"

Grace swallowed her mouthful of parsleyed broth. It was just a tad too salty, but fragrant with basil. It reminded her of a similar soup she had tasted in Montreal once. She nodded at Luke's question. "I can type with the best, for better or worse, and I knew the routine. In a year, I was helping to write the column, and gradually Mother began to enjoy her freedom, so she let me do more and more. She's quite the world traveler."

"And your father?" Luke asked. "Is he still around?"

"He's alive, if that's what you mean," Grace said, and she paused to take another dainty sip of soup. "Mother and Daddy don't communicate very often. They divorced many years ago. It was a terrible social scandal."

"Scandal? How come?"

"Divorce was a no-no among polite society. But Daddy was quite impossible, so Mother took the first step and got rid of him before he embarrassed her still more. He had some dreadful habits that Mother just couldn't cope with any longer. Gambling, for one. Heavens, why am I admitting such things to you?"

"I'll never repeat a word," Luke promised with a grin. "The proverbial gatepost and football players have similar IQs, y'know. What else?"

Just to tease him, Grace didn't rush to protest Luke's remark about his intelligence quotient. She smiled at him instead, and he grinned back at her, his eyes alight, understanding perfectly her unspoken barb about his brains—or lack of them. They shared a moment's silent laughter and then Grace went ahead with her confidences, saying lightly, "I suspect Daddy had other women as well, but of course I wouldn't dream of suggesting such a thing to Mother. He spent a great deal of time away from home at odd hours. Of course, I didn't blame him much. He liked to call Mother the Queen of the World, because of her ways. He's got deadly accuracy when it comes to name-calling."

Luke put down his spoon altogether, giving up on his soup and looking interested in the conversation. He rested his elbow on the edge of the table, then remembered himself and abruptly took it off again. "Do you communicate with him?" he asked.

Grace lifted her shoulders. "Daddy? Now and then.

Rarely, I suppose. He's quite a playboy, you see. His name is Harley Barrett. Being in football, you may have heard of him. He's a great sports fan."

"Harley Barrett?" Luke repeated softly, thinking hard and focusing on the tulips in the center of their table for a moment. Then his eyes widened a little and his dark head came up with a snap. "You don't mean Hedgehog Barrett, do you? Damn, I never made the connection! The guy who owns all those pizza parlors in the Midwest?"

Grace closed her eyes and pretended revulsion. "I believe he does own a few fast-food franchises, yes."

Luke cracked up laughing and nearly knocked over his wineglass. He rescued it swiftly and exclaimed, "I don't believe it! Hey, you're rich, Princess. Rollin' in dough, aren't you? Pizza dough, in fact."

Grace winced and begged, "Please!"

"Hedgehog Barrett," Luke repeated, looking at Grace with a new respect mixed with his laughter. "And you're his kid. How many brothers and sisters do you have to share it all with someday? Those pizza joints must be worth a fortune!"

"I have no intention of carrying on my father's business after he's gone," Grace said firmly. "I'm busy enough with my mother's! But to answer your question, I haven't any brothers or sisters."

"Yet," Luke added with devilish delight. "Last I heard, Hedgehog was goin' strong. Maybe you've got a baby brother somewhere in the world and just don't know it, Princess."

"I'm sure I would have received notice of a wedding," Grace said primly. Then, allowing a twinkle of her amusement to show, she added, "And Mother would have gotten the baby announcement. Daddy still loves to torment her."

"It sounds like that might be good sport," Luke agreed with a grin. "If you've got the reflexes to duck flying éclairs, of course. Ah, dinner. I'm starving."

He hadn't eaten his soup, though, and hadn't touched his roll—presumably because Grace hadn't partaken of *her* roll. Whether he was following her example of table manners or not, Grace wasn't sure. When the waiter had gone away, she began to eat with genuine hunger, and Luke did also.

Consuming her meal with precision, Grace began to ask tactfully about Luke's family. He had three brothers, he told her, all living outside St. Louis near the family homestead. All the brothers had gone to college on football scholarships, Grace learned, although Luke was the only one actually to finish all four years. He had gone to Notre Dame.

"Really?" she demanded, stunned.

Luke shrugged and claimed it was the truth, and he went on to say that his mother and father lived on a farm, but it had not been a working operation since his father had been wounded in Korea. A neighbor leased the fields from them and his mother raised a few chickens and a rare breed of goat, he explained, so the place still looked like the Kansas sets for *The Wizard of Oz*. Grace laughed, enjoying his descriptions and characterizations. He liked talking about his family, but he didn't volunteer much about himself, she noticed.

Finally, she finished her meal, and noted that Luke had eaten every bit of his entrée, right down to the sprig of parsley used to adorn the plate. He must have been starved! Grace declined dessert, thinking of her figure, but asked for a cup of espresso instead. Luke looked soulfully after the laden dessert cart with its delicacies in meringue and chocolate with dollops of whipped cream and garnishes of cleverly sugared fruit, but he refrained also. His sigh of longing was barely suppressed and positively comical to see. Grace didn't chide him. He'd behaved himself admirably without her interference.

She finished her drink and laid her napkin on the table. They were among the last patrons in the restaurant, and after he'd seen to the bill, Luke lounged gracefully beside her, his long legs extended out into the aisle between the tables for sufficient room to stretch. He was relaxed by this time, and he yawned suddenly, unable to stop himself. It was ten-thirty, Grace discovered with a glance at her watch.

"Goodness, it's late," she exclaimed. "You must be tired."

"I'm an early-to-bed person," Luke admitted, caught off guard by his own yawn. He visibly remembered his manners and sat up straight once again.

"And early to rise," Grace added kindly, with a smile for him. "I'd like to take a walk, to be honest. I'm not used to sitting still all day. Do you think I could?"

"I'll come with you," Luke said agreeably, getting up. He extended his hand to her and pulled her out of the banquette with so much force that she might have been sitting on a stadium bleacher. He steadied her while she caught her balance, and then he slid his hand under her elbow. "Do you walk every night?"

"I walk every day. Miles, it seems," she said, collecting herself. My, but it felt good to stand so close to him. Swallowing hard, she moved away and said, "I've missed the exercise since I've been on the road. Honestly, I don't mind going alone, if you'd rather not. I'm used to it."

"Walking alone in New York?" Luke questioned as they strolled across the restaurant carpet. "That kind of exercise must be more dangerous than dodging Oakland Raiders."

"Is that a football joke?" Grace laughed and shook her head. "I don't live in New York all the time, just two or three days a week. I have an apartment there, but I usually stay in Connecticut with Mother."

"At the baronial estate?" he asked archly.

"Something like that," Grace admitted with a smile, thinking of the spectacular Tudor-style mansion that Dear Mrs. Barrett had built. The Barretts were old money, and Mrs. Barrett's family, the Lendwells, were even snootier. Mrs. Barrett's home reflected her good breeding and good taste. Luke, with his down-home candor, would undoubtedly call the place a barn, for its airy, spacious rooms were sometimes drafty and cold with their Spartan modern decors. Grace preferred her small, homier apartment in the city, but it had been easier to collaborate on the column if she moved in with her mother again. However, Luke didn't need to hear about that.

In the lobby, they paused together with eerie synchronization and looked out through the glass doors into the

night. Grace realized the winter snowfall must be turning harsh again, for a gust of snow blasted along the
ice-encrusted panes. It had become an ugly night, and a
walk outdoors would be unpleasant.

"That's that," Luke said, and he tugged Grace away from
the door. "Do you want to get a drink instead? The bar's
probably open for a few more hours."

"I've had enough calories for one night. We may as well
call it a day. I've got to sort some laundry and send it out
in the morning, anyway."

"That's an excuse I haven't heard in a while," Luke
commented with a laugh. Then, as if catching himself, he
backtracked on the conversation, and as they headed for the
elevator together he asked quickly, "So why is a mature,
attractive lady like yourself cohabitating with her mother,
anyway? Can't be financial reasons. Are you a devoted
daughter, Princess?"

"Not overly devoted," Grace replied as they got onto the
elevator together. "We argue rather frequently, in fact."

"But always in good taste," Luke suggested, smiling
down at her.

"Always," Grace agreed wryly. "I'm not dependent on
Mother. At least, I don't think so. I've got my own circle
of friends, of course, and I still spend my social time in the
city."

"With Lucy," Luke guessed, remembering her friend.
"And this Kip character, I s'pose."

"Hmm," Grace said, shooting a sideways look up at him.
"You won't get me to talk about Kip tonight, thank you.
That subject is also off limits, Laser."

"Okay," he said amicably, shoving his hands down into
the front pockets of his jeans and rocking back on his heels
as the elevator ascended. Then he asked bluntly, "Were you
married to him?"

"No," Grace said, before she could stop herself.

"Engaged, I'll bet."

"I never gamble, so don't ask."

Luke nodded. "Engaged. I can tell by the way you flare

your nostrils when I ask the right question. You're a terrible liar."

Annoyance growing, Grace said, "I am not a horse. I do not flare my nostrils."

"Not a flare exactly, just a little twitch, I guess. Well? What happened? Kip dumped you? Or vice versa?"

The elevator doors parted, and Grace stalked off quickly. "I told you, I'm not going to talk about Kip."

"Kip," Luke said, trying out the sound of the name as he strolled in her wake. "Kip, Kipper, Kippy. What is that? Persian or something? It sounds like a puppy. Here, Kip. C'mere, boy." He whistled, as if expecting a cocker spaniel to come cavorting out from under the sofa.

"If you're trying to get me angry, you're succeeding." Grace put her handbag on the nearest table and kept walking toward her bedroom.

"Uh-oh. Are there any éclairs handy? Or am I safe?"

Grace spun around, her mouth pursed. "You know, you can be rather pleasant when you want to be. Why do you insist on acting like the stereotype of the moronic jock and spoiling everything?"

"Moronic is in the eye of the beholder," Luke shot back, his hands still hidden deep in his pants pockets. He smiled across the room at Grace, looking pleased with himself. "I thought it might help, that's all," he continued. "It's a sticky moment."

"What is a sticky moment?"

"Now," Luke explained agreeably. "Potential scoring situation. The fourth down and goal to go, you might say. I figured I'd get you riled up over your pal Kippy and you could go marching off to your room and slam the door. That way the pressure's off me."

"Are you speaking English?" Grace inquired, pretending ignorance as she retreated to the doorway of her bedroom.

Luke shrugged out of his jacket and tossed it haphazardly over the back of the sofa. Loosening his tie, he came around the furniture toward her. "Forgive the football metaphors. Look, we've hit it off pretty well, but we're coming up to the uncomfortable moment of deciding who is sleeping where, and I just thought that—"

"Oh, dear," Grace said, letting out a breath.

Luke went to the door of the other bedroom, tugging his tie out of his collar entirely. He unfastened the top button on his shirt and turned to look at her one last time. "I won't louse things up. Good night, Princess. Sleep tight."

With that, he went in and closed his door.

Grace glared after him. He was always getting the last word.

Dear Ms. Barrett,
I know that you say you're not an expert on un-requited love, but I hope you can help me. I'm sixteen years old and I've been admiring the son of my softball coach. The trouble is that he pretends I don't exist. Do you think he might be too shy to talk to me? What can a girl do to get a guy's attention if he doesn't want to give it?
—Getting Miffed in Milwaukee

Dear Mil,
Men don't like to risk humiliation. Don't get miffed with him—get clever. Your first option is to do what comes naturally. Speak casually with the young man, and hope that he soon catches on that you're inter-ested in more than talking softball scores. If that sub-tle, ladylike approach doesn't work, you can corner him in the dugout and confront him with your feelings. Do it politely, of course. Sometimes the shock value of honesty stirs men into behaving like gentlemen. They've got to understand that to ignore a lady is the worst insult of all.

CHAPTER SEVEN

GRACE SLEPT VERY badly and awoke much too early. Lifting her face out of her pillow, she glowered at her travel alarm, with its perky little clock face and bright gold hands that cheerfully announced seven-fifteen. It was Saturday morning, and she was awake at seven-fifteen!

Worse yet, she realized with a sudden wave of mixed emotions, it was Luke's voice that had brought her up from the depths of sleep. He was talking in the next room, softly but distinctly. He must be using the telephone.

Galvanized, Grace flung herself out of bed and raced lightfootedly to the vanity mirror. Hastily, she smoothed her tumbled hair. Not too smooth, of course. She didn't want Luke to think she *planned* to look beautiful for him. She bit her lips to give them some color and straightened the shoulders of her nightgown to allow the delicate folds of fabric to flow gracefully over her curves. There. All set.

Faking a feminine little yawn, Grace opened her bedroom door and glided out into the sitting room of the suite, her slender hand pressed daintily to her mouth.

Luke was indeed on the phone. He was half reclining on the pretty sofa, wearing nothing more than an abbreviated pair of tattered running shorts and some semiclean white athletic socks. His bare shoulders were thrown into dramatic relief by the slanting morning sunlight that shone through the tall windows. He had one large running shoe on his lap and he was struggling with a knot in the laces while pinning the receiver between his ear and naked shoulder. At Grace's entrance, he turned around and froze. He looked like an overgrown kid who had been caught with his paws in the cookie jar. When he met Grace's gaze, consternation showed clearly in his innocent blue eyes.

Whoever he was speaking to must have repeated a question, for Luke suddenly jumped and said into the receiver, "Uh, yes. And coffee, too . . . Fifteen minutes? Great. Yes, thanks."

He cradled the phone slowly, his eyes leaving Grace's face long enough to study her diaphanously concealed body. Holding his breath, he tipped his head sideways. He kept his mouth straight and appraised the length of her tall figure out of the corner of his eye, like a man who knows he shouldn't be looking but is unable to stop himself. He appeared to like what he saw, for the glimmer in his gaze was unmistakably male. Although he didn't smile, he showed all the signs of wanting to do just that.

Well, at least the look on his face was gratifying. Feeling suddenly quite naked, Grace hugged her own shoulders, temporarily hiding the fullness of her scantily clad breasts from him. She remembered her ruse and said, "Good morning. I thought you were still sleeping."

Luke shook his head slowly, still entranced by her appearance. "Not me."

Her own voice was still throaty with sleep, and she hoped that Luke didn't mistake the low, velvety sound of her words for seductive tones. She tried to sound brisk. "Of course. You've been out running."

"Not yet," Luke corrected, sitting up cautiously, as if any sudden move on his part might scare her away. "Just on my way out. You caught me."

"Yes, you looked like the picture of guilt when I came in. Exactly what are you up to?"

She didn't have to pretend curiosity. In fact, she was mystified by the collection of goodies he had spread out on the oval coffee table. Besides his headphones and small transistor radio, he also had an open carton of milk, a half-consumed package of Lorna Doones, the empty wrapper from some unsavory kind of junk food with a name that looked like Mr. Winky's Chocky Cake; however, Grace wasn't sure she was reading the cellophane lettering correctly. And in the crook of his elbow, Luke had an apple with a single chomp taken out of it.

Advancing on the oval table, Grace surveyed his cache and asked, "What is all this stuff? Your breakfast?"

Luke stayed on the sofa and bent his head. Perhaps he considered lying, but in the end he just sighed and came clean. "I can't help it. I was hungry last night."

"Last night?" Grace repeated.

Luke nodded stubbornly and didn't look up. "I went out again after you went to sleep."

"You went *out* for *food?*"

"Yes, dammit, and don't look shocked, please." Luke grabbed the apple in his hand and glared at it. "It's not like I let anybody see me do it, so your Dear Ms. Barrett reputation is safe. I had to go five blocks before I found an all-night market."

Grace dropped her arms and reached for the cellophane wrapper. Yes, it did indeed say Mr. Winky's Chocky Cake. A starving peasant from Outer Mongolia probably wouldn't touch such a thing, but a desperate football player had braved a blizzard to satiate himself. Grace couldn't stop her own smile. "There was no reason for you to go hungry, Luke."

"No?" he demanded bitterly.

Grace knelt beside the table and took inventory. Yes, he'd eaten half the package of his beloved Lorna Doones, and there was a plastic bag of fruit that looked fairly well depleted also. She smiled at his bent head. "That meal downstairs must have cost a fortune and you didn't eat half of it. Were you . . . ?"

"Afraid I was going to humiliate you and use a salad fork to stir my coffee?" he asked grudgingly, meeting her eyes. Bluntly, he answered his own question. "Yes."

Grace laid her hand on his bare knee and gave a sympathetic sigh. "You shouldn't have been self-conscious. I'm not a meter maid looking for violations, you know."

His gaze wavered once, sliding down to the curve of her breasts before snapping back up again. "N-no?"

"Of course not. If you're hungry, you should eat. Heavens, I don't want you to starve. You've been so nice to bring me here and spare me the ordeal of flying, the least I can do is let you eat your meals in peace."

Luke's hand stole around her wrist and held her lightly. "You don't owe me anything, you know. I came because I wanted to."

His grip was gentle but firm, and rather pleasant. Grace didn't shift away from him. On her knees beside the sofa, she could admire the strength of his upper body, the powerful breadth of his shoulders and the splendid contour of his chest. He had a light fuzz of curling hair there that formed a triangle, the two uppermost points being marked by his male nipples and then disappearing downward into his shorts. Relaxing like this, he exuded a passive strength that Grace found titillating. She unconsciously eased closer until her breast touched the hard length of his lower leg, then quaked at the resulting electrical sensation. Her hand lay on Luke's knee, her upper arm draping naturally along his thigh. He radiated a lovely warmth, but Grace felt her own skin rise up in excited prickles.

She couldn't help but see that Luke had two neat surgical punctures on his knee and another half-circle scar just above his kneecap on his thigh. She tore her gaze from the beautifully perfect shape of that thigh and tried to remember what he had just said to her. Giving herself a mental shake, she said just, as softly, "I'm glad you brought me here. I don't want to punish you for it, though. If you've got to eat, you've got to. Don't suffer anymore because of me, all right?"

He smiled a little. "All right."

"And I—I appreciate your honesty about this. It's good that you came right out and said that you were uncomfortable with me at dinner," Grace continued carefully. "I'm glad you could say exactly what was on your mind. Honesty's important."

Luke's thumb moved imperceptibly, caressing the underside of her wrist as if seeking her pulse there. Softly, he said, "Do you mean that?"

"Of course. I hope that we—that you can stop thinking I'm stuffy and be honest with me." She smiled tentatively. "I've got an open mind."

"How open?" Luke inquired, teasing gently. He leaned forward. His shoe slipped off his lap, but he proffered the unbitten side of his apple, holding the fruit just inches from Grace's nose. He said, "I can be awfully honest if I want to be."

He held the apple still. The temptation was too much, and Grace stretched upward, exposing her throat as she reached for the apple with her mouth. Both her breasts pressed firmly against his leg, and the static charge felt gloriously primitive. She couldn't hold Luke's gaze while she took a bite.

The apple was sweet and crisp and cleansing. It awakened her senses, it seemed. Grace smiled as she chewed it, enjoying the taste. Then she looked up at Luke, swallowed, and asked, "What do you want to be honest about? Something I've done?"

He shook his head. "Something *I haven't* done. Princess, I think I'd better set you straight before this gets out of hand."

Grace moved away abruptly, startled. "Before *what* gets out of hand?"

He held her wrist and didn't let go. "I've been lying to you. Sort of. By omission, I mean."

"About what?"

Luke leaned forward more, coming to sit on the edge of the sofa. He held the apple out. "Take another bite and listen. Princess," he said, after Grace had obeyed and bitten off a second portion of his apple. His voice was low, his eyes flickering. "I think you're gorgeous," he told her. "Your eyes are the color of a winter sky, and your mouth looks like it must taste better than just-picked fruit. You dress like a nun, and that's been driving me absolutely crazy. Sweet Judas, you even sleep covered from your chin to your toes. This nightgown looks like my grandmother's wedding dress."

Mouth full, Grace held her breath and watched his eyes like a fascinated mouse.

"And," he said clearly, "I want to undress you, to touch you and see if you're half as warm and soft as I think you are."

"But . . ." Grace began stupidly around her mouthful of apple.

"But nothing," Luke intervened gently. "I haven't got any kind of problem. Whatever you imagine is wrong with me isn't even remotely true. To be perfectly honest, I've been hot for you ever since you sat down in the back of that damned limo outside the Hilton. It's taken every ounce of willpower I possess to keep my hands off you."

Grace swallowed with difficulty. She noted dryly, "There's nothing wrong with your willpower, is there?"

He grinned. His heavy-lidded eyes looked sexy and warm, scanning the soft planes of her face. He lifted the apple, and with its unbroken side, he caressed a lazy circle on her cheekbone. The fruit felt cool and smooth against her skin. "I couldn't be sure of your reaction," he said. "I figured you'd slap me or kill me with one of your quick comebacks and I'd never get the chance to make love to you. And then the strategy started working in my favor."

"S-strategy?"

"I left you alone. I tried not to touch you, right?"

Grace tried to summon a glare. "Do you mean that you deliberately—"

"Began to tease you?" he interrupted. "Let you think you were going to help me overcome a terrible fear of women? It didn't start out that way. The idea that I had sexual problems came purely out of your own head." He grinned. "I had no calculated strategy to seduce you by indifference. But it certainly worked, didn't it?"

Grace glared at him in outrage. Of course, she could lie and tell him that she wasn't the least bit interested. Or she could smack his smiling face right now and end the discussion. She could pretend that he hadn't aroused her most womanly instincts and driven her to the point of dreaming about him both awake and asleep.

Dear Ms. Barrett,
If a man propositions me and I'd really like to accept, does proper etiquette say I must refuse?
                                                      —Kissed in Kalamazoo

Dear Kal,
In a word, no. Even Ms. Barrett knows that cutting off one's nose to spite one's face is a losing game.

Grace lifted her hand and took hold of the apple. Luke's fingers were strong beneath hers, but she pushed the apple to his mouth, indicating that it was his turn to bite it. When he did, she said bluntly, "Do you suppose you ought to cancel breakfast?"

Luke blinked and swallowed his mouthful whole. "Now?"

"Would you rather go running? Or into the next room with me?"

He was comically stunned by her direct approach. "Princess—you mean right now? This minute?"

"Here." Grace handed him the receiver and checked the printed directory for the room service number. She dialed the three digits. When the line began to ring, she moved to get up. She was bold, bolder than she'd ever been before. Her head was light already. Oh, murder. What was she doing? What was she *doing?*

Luke caught her wrist and held her still. He searched her eyes, scanned her face for signs of anger. Then the line clicked, and without looking away from Grace, he asked, "Room service? This is Lazurnovich again. Would you mind holding that order I just called in? For about an hour."

Grace held up two fingers.

"Uh," Luke said. "Make that two hours. Right. Thanks."

Grace hung up the receiver and pulled him to his feet. Don't lose the momentum now, she commanded herself inwardly. Don't blow it. Don't chicken out. This is it.

Luke didn't move, didn't draw her into his arms right away. He hesitated and asked, "Are you sure about this?"

Grace tipped her head up to him, her heart doing flip-flops in her chest. It was a nice question, she decided. He was asking her about her feelings now, not her hormones. A different kind of man would already have dragged her to the bedroom door. But Luke wanted her to be happy. He wanted her to enjoy what was coming and feel no recriminations. That one little question set him apart from most opportunistic men. And that was probably why she liked Luke the Laser so much. He wasn't just a brainless jock. He was a kind man, a gentle giant who really cared what she thought.

"No," she said honestly, without a smile, "I'm not sure. In fact, I'm almost certain I'm going to regret this very shortly. But I've never been a quitter. And I . . ."

"Yes?"

Grace took a steadying breath. "And I've never been attracted to anyone the way I am to you."

Luke touched his forefinger to the fabric of her night-gown at her shoulder. He traced the roundness of her flesh there and said, "That's the way I've been thinking, too, Princess. I don't spend a lot of time talking to the women I know, but I've had a good time with you. Talking, I mean. You're a good time."

He wasn't the type to get mushy, Grace decided. A "good time" was probably as high as a female got in the Laser's book. She cautiously touched his bare chest, conscious that her hand was trembling. His skin was warm, and she slipped her fingertips through the crisp tangle of hair there. "Thank you," she said, her voice shaky.

"And," he added deliberately, "I've been remiss. I haven't let you know how terrific you look, how you're the most *feminine* woman I've ever known. Princess, that quality turns me on so much! You're strong and intelligent, but not the least bit tough, and that ladylike side of yours fascinates me. I couldn't help wondering..."

He paused, as if unsure how she was going to react, and Grace promptly pressed, "What did you wonder?"

He slid his hand down her back, found the right spot on the curve of her spine to exert pressure, then pulled her whole body right into his. He bent and ran his nose through her hair. "Does a blue-blooded lady stay cool and quiet in bed? Or do you lose your head and get all hot and erotic?"

Grace laughed, although the sound shivered and evaporated. Luke's mouth had found the crest of her ear, and he breathed a soft breath there. His tongue made a cat-stroke caress, melting her entirely. With difficulty, she reprimanded, "Sometimes, Laser, you're really disgusting."

He gathered her up in his arms, sensuously drawing her body to his so that the silky material of her nightgown was the only meager barrier between them. He seemed to relish the softness of her breasts against his hard chest. "Exactly what about me do you find disgusting?" he questioned. "What I'm wearing isn't going to hide anything in about five more seconds, so you could get a real shock if—"

Grace laughed softly. He was adorably sweet, after all. She wrapped her arms around him, running her hands up the muscles of his back and down again. "It's not your body that's disgusting. How can a man be so lovely to look at, Laser?"

He found her throat with his lips, sending rockets of pleasure shooting through her veins. Chuckling against her warm skin, he answered as if conducting an interview, "Well, Howard, it's taken years of practice, but I find that the best way to get a woman's attention is to take off all my clothes in the first six minutes after we've met. When she's blinded to my intellectual inadequacies, I move in for the kill—"

"I don't think you're intellectually inadequate," Grace said, interrupting. And then she gasped, for Luke had skillfully slipped his hand around to cup her breast from underneath. His thumb sought the nipple there, and the white-hot flush of excitement caught her like a cresting wave. She wanted him so much that her legs were weak and wobbly all of a sudden. His mouth, his hands, his whole body, had aroused her in the space of a few seconds. Never mind that he was charmingly sincere, shyly delighted. Luke was a sexy man who undoubtedly possessed the expertise to drive a woman crazy with passion. Shaking, Grace began, "Luke, I'd like . . ."

"Yes," he said firmly, understanding her message. He slid one arm around her shoulders to guide her and moved around the sofa, drawing her gently along with him.

Her bedroom door was still open, and they were inside at once. The room was not dark, for the curtains were parted just a few inches to allow the morning light to penetrate. The fluorescent light from the bathroom also spilled into the room. It was just the way Grace wanted. No groping in the darkness would satisfy her now.

Luke drew her to the bedside and turned her away from him, then brought up his hands to unfasten the button at the nape of her neck. With that undone, he filled his hands with the silken texture of her hair. Softly, he murmured, "Beautiful." Then he passed his hands lovingly down her back until he found the soft curve of her bottom through the fabric. He sighed tightly.

Grace smiled at the sound. Finally, he was demonstrating that he found her attractive. Not just attractive, but very sexy. She slipped her arms out of the nightgown. Momentarily shy, she held the filmy garment to her breasts. This wasn't the way Grace Barrett usually behaved. In fact, this was so far from normal that Grace abruptly relished the role of a different woman. She was new, a woman who had captured the attention of Luke "the Laser" Lazurnovich, and that thought was strangely exciting. She leaned back against him, eyes closed as he caressed her. His hands roamed eagerly around her hips, across her belly, and then up to capture her breasts once more. His touch was sure and skillful yet slow, as if he was truly appreciating her lines and curves. Grace felt happy and female as he learned the intricacies of her tall, slender body.

Slowly, she let the nightgown slip lower. With her back bare, she leaned against him once more. She could feel the heat of his arousal against her bottom, and that proof of his delight brought her more pleasure. She let her nightgown fall altogether, and it slipped soundlessly to the floor. Then, naked, she turned to Luke's body, sliding her arms around his neck.

He found her mouth with his. This time, his kiss wasn't rushed, but slow and measuring. Against hers, his lips felt hot with barely suppressed excitement, but he was gentle. He parted her mouth with an authoritative nudge, then brushed her tongue with his. He plunged deeper, tasting the apple sweetness of her and exchanging that subtle essence with his own. Grace aligned her body with his, stretching high on tiptoe to press close. She linked her fingers behind his head, weaving the brown curls there so she held him inescapably. Teasing then, she arched her slim body to provoke his passion.

Luke tore his mouth from hers long enough to gasp a tortured laugh and beg, "Prin-cess!"

Smiling, Grace slid her hands down his torso. His muscle was like fine, warm oak, but his skin seemed to shiver under her touch. He wasn't calm and collected. At her caress, he responded just as swiftly as she had. She found the rigid undulation of his ribs and the way his muscle-taut lower back fit smoothly into his hips. Palms down, she eased her hands inside his running shorts, inside his underwear. He twisted imperceptibly, his breath tight in his chest. Hooking her thumbs over his waistband, she tugged gently downward. Luke pulled her head to his for another long, savoring kiss, and she used the moment to draw off his clothes.

An instant later, they were naked and kissing wildly, mouths parted, tongues slick and seeking, arms pressing each other to the melding point. Grace's pulse skyrocketed and her breath came fast and raggedly. Luke was warm and hard, yet fit her every curve exquisitely. He smelled of soap and apples and that spicy-salty scent that was so uniquely, so wonderfully, his own. Grace's head was full of the sensations but weightless with delight. Her body reacted with waves of hot, shivery desire.

Luke felt her shudder of excitement and absorbed it. Against her lips, Grace felt him smile. She knew that he liked the way she was slowly stripping off her own inhibitions. She didn't think of her Dear Ms. Barrett persona. For the moment, all she wanted was to be a woman who could please and take pleasure willingly.

CHAPTER EIGHT

ON THE BED, Luke turned very gentle. Perhaps he was afraid he might hurt her, and under different circumstances, Grace might well have been afraid. He was awfully big, weighing almost twice what she did, she guessed. And his carefully controlled strength was obvious when he rolled her onto her belly and kneaded the tension from her back. He stroked her buttocks, enjoying the length of her smooth thighs, and rolled her again to curl her supple leg around his hip. He controlled her, experimented with her, all the while teasing and pleasing. He heard her almost inaudible gasps and quickly repeated the caress until Grace responded anew.

There was little haste in Luke's exploration, and yet Grace was breathless and panting in no time. When he nuzzled her throat, licked her nipples, and then moved lower to kiss the smooth surface of her belly, she grasped his head and writhed with pleasure. A moan escaped her lips when his hand delved between her thighs and found the warm center where the evidence of her womanly excitement was moist and waiting. She parted her thighs and tried to encourage him to settle there and end her torment.

But Luke was careful, cautious of her delicate bones and feminine vulnerability. He lay back and encased her in his arms. Kissing her throat and face, he rolled her on top of him. Grace rejoiced in the tenderness of his actions. He was very gentle, although she judged by the quickness of his breathing and the careening heartbeat pulsing against her own breast that he found great excitement in her body. She smiled and teased his chest with her lips and tongue, then licked his nipples, giggling when he grabbed her head to stop her. Time stretched immeasurably while they explored and shared.

Then Luke drew her face to his and pressed another seething, communicative kiss to her lips, and Grace eased lower until the hottest part of him met the welcoming warmth of her own body. With a groan, he arched upward, seeking swiftly to end his own inner turmoil.

Grace yielded with alacrity. She found him and sank slowly, tantalizingly, down onto him until he was firmly inside her. She held her breath. He felt as hot as summer sunbeams, awakening sensations inside her that soon flourished and bloomed. An intense quiver began to flutter within her almost as soon as Luke found her most secret depth. At first he felt hard, almost hurting, within her, but she quickly recognized the real urgency in herself. She shuddered at the quickening sensation where her flesh met his so firmly. She couldn't stop her own murmur of relief and excitement. "Oh, Luke."

Luke didn't move, but held very still within her. His fingertips traced swirls of sensual messages along her back. His breath was uneven at her ear. "You're so good, so sweet, Princess."

Grace moved above him, withdrawing the wondrous pleasure for an instant and then pressing down once more until she was brimming with him. Again and again she brought him snugly inside her. Then he pushed her up to sit above him. With his passion-lazy eyes watching hers, he caressed her belly and stroked her breasts, nipping their excited peaks with his fingers. Next he cupped her bottom, guiding her swiftly first, then slowly, to suit himself, but always with a fluent, rhythmic grace, and finally with an intensity both deep and powerful. Grace arched against him and cried out involuntarily. The fluttering inside her own body turned to roiling pleasure with each thrust. Her heart drummed. She threw back her head and gasped for cooling breath, but the storm inside was too much.

"Look at me now," Luke protested breathlessly. He controlled her wild tempo momentarily with his strong hands. "Don't shut me out, Princess."

She obeyed, biting her lip and seeking his vivid blue eyes with her own. He seemed to see into her mind then, and she into his. The message was clear and carnal, yet tempered with deep, unspoken emotion. With their souls suddenly locked together in that electric moment, Luke thrust and ignited a sudden, flaring fireball inside her. Grace squeezed and trembled, and finally gave a wrenching, uncontrolled cry: "Luke!"

He seethed inside her, holding her body fast to his for one final, mighty thrust. Grace burst over the edge of ecstasy and melted, melded, welded, to Luke's strength and power. She heard him echo her abandoned cry with a deep growl that signified his own release. They were taut together in a shimmering moment of perfect intimacy. Then Luke, recovering his sense of reality first, gathered her soothingly to his chest, and they clung to each other in sated exhaustion.

Only then did Grace's mind register what had just passed between them. With Luke she had made a new kind of love, a spontaneous act of passion, a miraculous joining of spirit and body of a depth and completeness she had never experienced with Kip. Although she had known Kip for many, many years and had understood his personality and his moods, she had never reached such heights of sexual pleasure with him. This was different. Luke was different.

Not only was he a proficient lover, but he gave himself naturally, without inhibition. He hadn't fussed about the details, the individual caresses, the taking turns in passive and aggressive roles. He had shared himself, this big, sometimes enigmatic man, and he had wanted nothing less in return. He had relished each new plane of passion as they gained it and sought to find her profound woman's spirit. Even now, he was absorbing her warmth, enjoying the fulfilled lassitude of her body covering his, and inhaling the fragrance of her hair as it tumbled about their heads. His hands lay quietly on her back, but Grace knew they were alive to her slightest breath, her smallest movement.

"Grace," he murmured finally, as if dedicating the word to the beauty of the act they had just experienced. He had never said her name before, and the sound of it brought a rush of tender feelings to Grace's throat. Never had her name sounded so poignant.

She almost cried. But that would have been too unbearable. Grace knew she was capable of giving only a limited amount of herself to this almost-stranger even now, after their shattering lovemaking. She controlled herself and laid her hand on the powerful rise of his chest. Smiling, she traced her fingertip through the fuzzy hair there. "At least you got the name right."

He laughed a little and hugged her lightly. "I knew it all along. It hasn't quite suited you until now. You're not stiff and stuffy, after all, but alive and graceful."

"Not as much as you," Grace said softly, glad she could hide her eyes from him at this moment. Somehow, this quiet talk was even more intimate than the physical climax just moments before. She explained, "You're beautiful."

"I know, I know. Adonis in a size-thirteen sneaker, right?"

Grace giggled and pressed her cheek to his chest. "That's not what I meant. You're not—not the least bit what I thought football was all about."

"Brute force?" Luke asked, and she could hear the smile in his voice. He caressed his way down her spine with feather-soft fingertips as if her back were a pearl-studded ribbon. He agreed, saying, "I've always been known for my finesse."

Grace gave a contented little purr, like a satisfied cat. Then she sighed. "I adore finesse."

Luke caught her chin with his forefinger. Tenderly, he

lifted her face until they were eye to eye once more. His gaze was flickering again, and his mouth curved into a lazy half-smile that made Grace's heart turn over with a great ker-thump. He drew her to his lips and murmured, "I think I could learn to adore you."

He kissed her softly, gently, like the merest butterfly wings on a sun-sweet surface. Grace felt her eyelids burn, and she didn't dare let him see her reaction. He could melt an igloo, she thought distantly. He could turn a woman to maple syrup if he wanted to. How had she stumbled on this perfect man?

After a time, he rolled her onto her side in the bed and petted her in silence, his forehead and nose whimsically touching hers all the while. She had only to open her eyes now and then to absorb the warmth of his gaze. Grace felt her breathing return to normal. Without urgency, she touched his body, exploring in calmer times what she had only briefly excited during their heated lovemaking. She explored and gave him gentle pleasure, the kind they had hastily forgone before. With drowsy sensuality, they lay together in the tangled sheets.

Eventually, they were both all but asleep, luxuriating in a cocoon of contentment and delicious, newfound closeness.

Unfortunately, the phone rang and shattered their golden bliss. Grace jumped, startled, and while Luke lay smiling and obviously prepared to ignore the call, she reached for the night table and fumbled with the receiver. "This is probably room service," she told him as she sat up.

"Tell them another two hours."

Tugging the sheet to her bare breasts in an absurd attempt at modesty, Grace answered the call. "Hello?"

Lucy Simons's voice sounded blunt and suspicious to Grace's ear. Lucy said darkly, "I have tracked you down like those slavering bloodhounds in *Uncle Tom's Cabin*. Darling Gray, are you doing what I think you're doing?"

"What do you think I'm doing, Lucy?" Grace asked, matching her friend's calm voice. With Luke here beside her, Grace smiled broadly at the sound of Lucy's familiar sarcasm, and laid a hand on Luke's bare chest. He picked up her wrist and feigned biting her on the arm. Drawing her arm with him, he rolled over and pretended to go to sleep, supposedly giving her some privacy for her telephone call. He hugged her hand to his heart and kept it warm.

Lucy said, "I talked with every desk clerk in that town until I found one who thought he recognized Dear Ms. Barrett. He squealed on you and your friend. I think you're shacking up with a man with a multisyllabic Polish name."

"It's not Polish. At least, I don't think it is. It's Lazurnovich."

"Hmm," Lucy said dryly. "He sounds like a hockey player."

"Wrong again," Grace countered lightly. "Football."

"You're *jesting!*" Lucy exclaimed in disbelief, abandoning her Fran Lebowitz routine. "Gray Barrett! A *football* player? Not really!"

"A Pittsburgh Steeler," Grace said smugly, as with her free hand she plumped her pillow and settled back in comfort. Luke tipped his head and opened one eye curiously, so Grace seized the opportunity and asked him, "Wide receiver, right?" Luke nodded and rolled away again, and Grace said into the phone, "Yes, a wide receiver. That's the fellow who catches the ball."

"My God, pass me the vodka," Lucy said prayerfully.

"You're being melodramatic, Luce."

"Amen! I've got cause! I'm trying to imagine what your aunts on Long Island are going to say. They're going to need smelling salts, and your mother will have to go into seclusion or something. Gray, please. She's already giving me the devil for making you go for so long!"

"Do you think she's going to blame you for my indiscretions?" Grace grinned at the thought. "I may not straighten her out, Luce. You can take the heat for once. Has she been calling you?"

"Well," Lucy admitted reluctantly, "yesterday was the first time. Gray, you know she is not going to tactfully welcome a wide receiver into the family's hallowed halls. Forgive me for asking, darling, but have you lost your *mind?* Your mother will have a fit!"

"Good. She needs to have her circulation stirred up a bit, I think. I'm certainly discovering that it does wonders."

"Spare me the erotic details of lovemaking," Lucy commanded dismally. "At least, not at this hour of the morning. Wait until we're alone together over two very large Bloody Marys."

"We'll see about that," Grace retorted, for she had soon regretted confiding in Lucy about her troubles with Kip. "You may try to blackmail me later, if I'm not careful," she told Lucy, then asked, "What did Mother want? Is she looking for me? She already has my itinerary."

"Which you seem to be ignoring," Lucy snapped. "What is the hotel you're staying in now, may I ask? Has the football player taken you someplace horribly common?"

"On the contrary, it's fabulous." Grace glanced around the luxurious room with its art deco appointments and beautifully subtle color scheme. She said, "I may take his advice from now on, in fact."

"My God," Lucy said violently, "do you mean you intend to continue traveling with him? Gray! *Really?* Is this true love or something? Or the most delicious sex you've ever had and now you can't live without it?"

"Shut up, Lucy," Grace said with a laugh, suddenly full of good humor. "I haven't decided yet. I'm going ahead with the tour, of course. Detroit next, right?"

"Yes," Lucy said distractedly. "Let me check my notes. Has Vince Lombardi got a hotel in mind?"

"Even I know that Vince Lombardi was a coach," Grace said with sudden irritation.

"And he played defense at Fordham," Lucy came back promptly. "Don't I amaze you sometimes?"

"Frequently," Grace said dryly. Dropping her voice, she added, "Look, I may be alone. I don't—I'm not sure what's going on yet, all right? I'll stick with my hotel reservations from now on, I promise. You're picking up the tab, aren't you?"

"The publisher will not be amused to find that we're paying for romantic trysts in half the cities in the country, but yes, I'll pay the tab, whether or not you've got a roommate." Lucy's voice became serious when the talk shifted to business. Although Lucy was first Grace's friend, second she was a very professional publicist. Briskly, she said, "By the way, I've got some things to send to you, so I'll forward them to the Detroit hotel. Ask at the desk. Your syndicate has a packet for Dear Ms. Barrett, too. Is there anything else you need? Clothes? Note pads? Contraceptives?"

"You're being very catty," Grace noted cheerfully. "No, I don't need anything."

"Except your sanity," Lucy shot back. "Oh, hell, scratch that comment. I'm glad you're breaking out of your shell, to be honest. You've been acting like the ugly duckling for too long. Good for Lombardi, if he's the cause of this switch. Listen, Gray, the purpose of my call was actually to inform you of your mother's plans."

"Uh-oh."

"Calm yourself, darling. She wants to throw a party."

Grace slumped against the pillow. "Oh, murder!"

"Relax. It's a great idea. We think the book's going to hit the best-seller lists by the end of next week. We should definitely celebrate, and your mother, the sweet thing, has decided to give a party."

"You're calling her sweet because she's paying for it, right?"

"Precisely. It's a marvelous idea, and the publicity could be wonderful if we play our cards right. I've got to figure out some kind of angle between now and then that will draw national publicity. Some kind of stunt, I think, but it's got to be tasteful without being outlandish. Colorful, yet classy. Any ideas?"

"Creative party-giving was never my strong suit. For when and where is it planned?"

"Dallas," Lucy said succinctly. "The last stop on your tour. We're going to meet you there and have a real blowout that will attract even the television networks. And I'm working on the guest list now. Besides the press, whom would you like me to invite?"

"Oh, Lucy, that's your department, not mine."

"Kip?"

"Lord, no!"

"Aha," Lucy said wisely. "Lombardi?"

Grace still had her hand imprisoned in Luke's and pressed against the heat of his chest. Grace smiled down at his snoozing profile. "Yes, please, Lucy."

"Good," Lucy said, and she must have made a note with her pencil. "I'll send his invitation to Detroit. It will be an invitation-only party, so pin it to his jersey to make sure he doesn't lose it before then."

"You just wait," Grace promised. "Your jaw is going to drop, Lucille."

Lucy undoubtedly grinned, for there was a short silence before she asked, "He's a real hunk, huh?"

"Yes."

"And a honey, too?"

"Definitely a sweetheart, Lucy."

"True love?"

Grace sighed and gazed down at Luke's inert but splendid body. Without thinking about it, she bent closer and nuzzled playfully across his warm shoulder and down into the crook of his neck. Against her fingertips, she could feel his steady pulse, and she smiled thoughtfully. The man definitely had heart. He had turned his face into the pillow and looked charmingly sweet as he dozed beside her. To Lucy, Grace said softly, "Perhaps, Lucy, dear. Perhaps."

"Hmm," Lucy said gruffly. "Well, enjoy it while it lasts. Will you call me when you get to Detroit?"

"Of course."

"All right. Give Lombardi a kiss for me. Perhaps even a little pat on the fanny. Football players do that all the time, don't they? Yes, give him one of those casual little smacks from me. I'll try one in person in Dallas."

"Good-bye, Lucy."

"Yes, Gray. Good-bye."

When Grace turned away to cradle the phone again, Luke rolled over and locked his arm around her body. Diving under the sheet, he found her breast with his lips again, teasing her. Then pressed her back into the pillow.

Grace laughed and lay back beneath him, filled with

sudden delight once more. "Are you awake after all? Ready for breakfast yet?"

"No," Luke said from under the sheet. "Call room service back. Cancel breakfast altogether, all right?"

CHAPTER NINE

ON SATURDAY EVENING Grace was scheduled to appear live on a short evening television talk show, and then she had to do a radio call-in program later that same night. Aside from those few hours, she hardly left the hotel suite that weekend.

In fact, she hardly left the bedroom.

After sleeping late on Sunday morning, Grace confronted the moment of truth as she stepped out of the shower, her wet hair bound up in a towel. Luke wore a white towel clasped around his trim hips as he shaved at the bathroom mirror. He was apparently enjoying her reflection, because he was taking a very long time at the steamy mirror and repeatedly stopped to wipe it clear with his palm. As he rinsed his razor under the tap, he asked casually, "What time do you have to be in Detroit?"

"Eleven A.M. tomorrow," she told him, wrapping a lush bath towel around her wet body. "I've got a hotel reservation there for tonight.

Luke picked up his watch from the counter and took a

look at the time. Then he put the watch down again and resumed shaving. "When do we leave?" he said.

Grace went very still behind him. Cautiously, she asked, "We?"

"You heard me," Luke said, and he carefully shaved his throat in slow upward strokes.

"Are you—are you coming with me?" she asked, shaken.

"You don't plan on flying, do you? How else are you going to get there, Princess?"

Grace let out an unsteady breath in relief. She'd been terrified that he wasn't going any farther than Cincinnati. There wasn't any reason for him to go to Detroit—not really. Once they'd slept together, he might have easily decided to head back to Pittsburgh, mission accomplished. That he wanted to stay with her told Grace a great deal, but not enough.

Hopefully, this was more than a mere sexual odyssey for Luke. It had certainly turned into a self-revealing journey for Grace. She didn't want to leave him yet. There was too much she still didn't know and understand about Luke the Laser. And too much to discover within herself. She wasn't accustomed to giving her body without sharing some all-important words first. With Luke, there hadn't been time. Or maybe she had fallen into a purely sexual relationship for the first time in her life. Grace didn't want to think that was true. She leaned weakly against the shower door and began to unwind the towel from her hair to conceal her sudden emotional moment from Luke.

"I think it would be smart to get on the road before too long," he said, turning on the tap again. He eyed her in the mirror, and Grace quickly tried to collect herself. She didn't want him to think she was upset.

"We may as well travel in daylight," Luke added, sounding suspiciously serious. "Unless, of course, you're afraid someone's going to see us and report your appalling choice of lover to your mother."

With a shout of outrage, Grace swatted him with her towel. Luke yelped and laughed, and she knew he'd joked her out of her tense moment. The discussion was over.

* * *

The drive to Detroit was fun. Between frequent stops for snacks to placate his ever-grumbling stomach, Luke turned the radio on full blast, enjoying the tunes from Motown. Grace got a foolish kind of delight from listening to him sing. He didn't sing badly, in fact. His high notes warbled a bit, but his Barry White low notes weren't bad at all. Grace laughed and joined in, singing along on the well-known choruses of some Gladys Knight oldies. Harmonizing on "I Heard It Through the Grapevine," they roared into Detroit.

The hotel was big and impressive, and after they were settled in a suite that lacked the luxurious beauty of the Omni Netherland Plaza but made up for the lack of ambience with plenty of space and a complimentary bottle of champagne, Luke got on the telephone. He was munching an apple from his limitless supply while the line rang, and Grace was shaking out her wardrobe and carefully hanging her dresses in the closet.

"Giz?" Luke asked when his call connected. "I don't believe you're still at that number! Yeah, it's the Laser."

Grace, having no scruples about eavesdropping as Luke had when Lucy called, listened unabashedly. Whoever Giz was, he seemed to be delighted to be hearing from Luke the Laser. Luke hardly got a word in.

"Okay," Luke said, and he listened some more. Then his voice rose in excitement. "Yeah? When? No! He's Dead? Man, that's great! What time? Sure, there's a lady involved. I think she can handle it. Are you planning to get naked in the first hour? All right, I'll bring her, then. Count on it. Later."

Luke hung up the phone and cackled with pleasure. He spun around in a real Motown move, tossed his apple up into the air, and caught it deftly once again with his other hand. He took another noisy bite.

"What was that all about?" Grace asked, noting his delight. "Surely someone hasn't died?"

Luke danced over to her, smiling. "You won't believe it. A bunch of friends of mine are havin' a party tonight."

"Friends?" Grace asked cautiously. "Having a party after a funeral?"

"Who said anything about a funeral? Wait and see, Princess. Trust me, you'll love it." He swooped in and gave her a wet kiss on the mouth. His eyes were sparkling as he gathered her up in his arms. "This is going to be a real cultural exchange, Princess. Have you got something glittery to wear?"

"Glittery?" Grace asked with disdain, trying to hold back her smile as she looped her arms around his neck. He looked so happy when he was enjoying himself that it was hard not to laugh with him. "Do you mean diamonds?"

"No, no, no. Like sequins. Or feathery stuff. Or satin pants." Still holding her against his body, he began to file through the hangers she had already meticulously placed in the closet the required two inches apart to prevent wrinkling. The hangers clattered together under Luke's manhandling, and his half-eaten apple left a wet swath on her red silk blouse. "Anything like that in here?"

Grace tried to push free of him to rescue her clothing. "As a matter of fact, I don't own a single sequin, Laser. Will you get out of there, please? If I'm going to a party, I'll choose my own outfit!"

Luke groaned. "Just don't look like you're headed for a garden-club tea, huh? This is a special occasion."

"I think I know how to dress appropriately. Can you give me a clue as to what the other women will be wearing?"

Luke lifted his nose to taunt Grace, pantomiming her superior attitude and snooty tone of voice. "If memory serves, my dear Ms. Barrett, the women don't usually wear *anything* at these parties. Think you'll fit in?"

Grace sputtered and fought to get free of him. Luke laughed and ended up catching her around the waist and dragging her to the bedside. His kiss quickly distracted Grace from any thoughts of fighting. They made love for about the dozenth time in two days, and she had to take a nap to recover.

Luke insisted they have dinner before the party.

"I feel as though I've been eating constantly all day," Grace objected when he started to call room service. "I think I'll just have a snack at the party instead, all right?"

Luke shook his head and dialed. "There won't be any food there."

"Really? I can't imagine a party for men like you without snacks to keep you from rioting."

Luke shrugged. "There got to be too many food fights, so we outlawed it."

"Food fights?" That bit of information brought Grace up short. "Just exactly who is going to be at this party? King Kong's little brothers?"

"No, no, just a bunch of the guys. Football players." Luke's grin was one of unholy mirth. "We're gonna test that open mind of yours, Princess."

With growing trepidation, Grace got dressed for the party.

Luke knew the way, so he drove them to a splendid house in the middle of a respectable-looking suburban neighborhood. But when he pulled her out of the Jaguar, Grace could hear the music, even though they were still half a block from the front door. She took Luke's arm and clung tightly as they walked along the snowy sidewalk.

"Just stick close, all right?" he said when they had reached the front porch. "Don't wander off and get into trouble."

"Yes, sir," Grace replied with mock demureness.

Luke didn't bother with the doorbell. He shouldered the front door open and pulled her inside.

The music was thumping, bellowing rock'n'roll that assaulted Grace's eardrums like amplified jungle tom-toms. She winced and refrained from clapping her hands over her ears. The foyer was spacious, but already crowded with brightly dressed people in various sizes, shapes, and colors. A huge black man disengaged himself from the amorous embrace of a satin-clad young woman and advanced on Grace and Luke with a grin on his face. He was dressed in a very posh cashmere sweater and tailored trousers, but his head sported a ridiculously tiny beany hat that read: MOTOWN

AMATEUR OPEN—TAG TEAM. Grace couldn't begin to guess what kind of golf tournament might require the services of tag teams.

"The Laser! My main man! Hey, bro, howya been?"

"Gizmo!" Luke shouted above the music. They clasped hands and then flung themselves into each other's arms. Since Gizmo was several inches taller than Luke and at least fifty pounds heavier, the sight was awesome.

Gizmo pounded Luke's back with pleasure. "Man, I haven't seen you since Speeder's wedding! Howya been? Who's your lady? Man, ain't she something out of Park Avenue!"

Grace tried not to blush. Her wool dress, a tasteful garment in voile that was precisely the red-gold shade of a Latour claret, enhanced her coloring and suited most occasions from wakes to commencements and evenings after the theater. With a pearl pendant, she had thought she looked dressy and attractive, but after glancing around at the mixture of guests, she could see she had guessed wrong. Gizmo stared at her as if she were a Monet painting in a graffiti display.

"Giz, this is Grace," Luke introduced, not noticing Grace's immediate discomfort. "She's visiting from New York. Grace, meet the great Gizmo Montgomery, a Hall of Fame linebacker, believe it or not. Used to be with the Lions."

"How do you do?" Grace said, extending her hand.

At her display of good manners, Gizmo's eyes popped in amazement, and he looked at Luke. "Where did you get this one, my man? This is amazin'! Amazin' Grace! That's it. My, my, you sure look juicy, Amazin' Grace. Where'd did you come from, lady?"

"From New York," Grace said composedly, although her small hand had been squeezed lifeless in Gizmo's gigantic one.

"New York, New York," Gizmo said, shaking his head in admiration as he looked her up and down. "My, my, things have been changin' for the better in the Big Apple! The question is, how'd you end up with the likes of the Laser? Those smooth moves of his are still smooth, huh?

Laser, take this fine lady inside for a drink. Get her some of the good stuff, mind you. He's Dead went back in the kitchen, I think."

Luke made a grab for Grace's hand. "Let's go."

"Who's dead?" Grace asked in alarm.

The music got louder, so Luke couldn't hear her. He caught the *wh-wham wh-wham* beat of the rock'n'roll and danced along the hallway, weaving through the throng there, dragging Grace along behind. She made sure she hung on to his hand tightly. She didn't want to get lost in this!

Manly shouts erupted when Luke pushed through a swinging door to the kitchen, and his hand was torn from hers. Luke was engulfed in a horde of huge men, and Grace shrank back against the door for safety's sake. The men shouted and thumped each other's back and laughed and swore and generally expressed delirious happiness at finding themselves together again. One man with a close-cropped Afro and a nose that had been flattened almost entirely expressed his joy by grabbing a beer can from a Styrofoam cooler. In exultation, he drained its contents in four huge swallows and threw the empty can out onto the dining-room floor. He reached for another and tossed it end over end at Luke.

Luke caught it with the nimble expertise of a man accustomed to catching flying objects, and then he remembered Grace. He dived for her again, and tugged her by the hand into the fray.

"Hey, hey," he called, getting everyone's attention. "I want you to meet someone. This is Grace. Grace, this is Leon Murzowski and Blood Mitchell. She's a writer, Blood, so watch your language."

The man-mountain called Blood snorted an expletive, so Luke gave him a rabbit punch in the stomach, and he doubled over and faked agony.

"And this," said Luke, turning to the last enormous football player, "is my greatest enemy on earth, He's Dead Jim McCoy. Say hello to the lady."

Grace found herself shoved to stand directly in front of a fire hydrant of a man. He was just Luke's height, but built like a bullterrier, with a huge neck, gigantic torso, and too-short but powerful-looking legs. He was wearing a Hawaiian flowered shirt that was stretched so tightly across his belly that the buttons might well have been screaming. His face was as pink as a cherub's, but his eyes were dangerously black in color and very arresting. His cheek bulged with chewing tobacco. Grace didn't dare hold out her hand in greeting.

He's Dead Jim McCoy didn't crack a smile. Glowering at Grace out from under thick, threatening eyebrows, he looked up and down her figure insolently, judging. Finally, he nodded once, like a Syndicate don. "Ver-ry nice, Laser. Ver-ry nice. Great legs, huh? Does she put out?"

The rest of the men burst out laughing and Grace flushed. Luke pulled her back against his body, but he was laughing also. "Do you think I'd tell you, you perverted boar?"

Lightning fast, He's Dead Jim McCoy shot out a hand and cracked Luke a glancing blow across the side of his head. Then he laughed, too, and shoved himself off the table where he'd been relaxing. "Get the lady a beer, you sons of Eskimo lard!" he bellowed.

Knowing her eyes were round as soup plates, Grace turned quickly into Luke. "Why do you call him that name?"

"He's Dead Jim?" Luke asked.

"Easy," said Leon Murzowski explained, handing Grace a can of beer. "Remember *Star Trek*? The TV show?"

"The starship doctor was called McCoy, but he didn't have a very big part in the show," Luke intervened. "In every episode, his big line was the same. He'd crouch down over the body of some other character and look up at Captain Kirk and say, 'He's dead, Jim.' That was the only line he ever needed to learn."

Grace looked warily at He's Dead Jim McCoy. "So that's why you call him that?"

He's Dead laughed unpleasantly. "There's more. That's the only line the refs ever had to say to me. I'd knock some poor toad on his back and the ref would come over and look at the guy I'd hit and say, 'He's dead, Jim.' Easy."

Grace shuddered, and at her reaction the men broke up laughing again.

They slapped hands all around and quaffed their beer and exchanged more sensible greetings and gossip, such as who was living where and how business was going, and who was the kid from Notre Dame this year who was something called a first-round draft choice. As she listened Grace soon decided that the men were all retired football players, and they had played for a variety of teams. Leon Murzowski, also known as the Reverend, for instance, had been a teammate of Luke's at Notre Dame who had played for the Detroit Lions before retiring and going into the insurance business. Blood, an enormous and frighteningly silent black man, had gone to high school in Georgia, played football at some southern college, the name of which Grace didn't catch, and then had been a tackle for the Los Angeles Rams. He's Dead Jim McCoy had gone to that same Georgia high school, but he'd gone to college in Nebraska and finally played safety for Detroit.

"I didn't think fraternization between enemy camps was very likely," Grace observed when someone asked her what she thought of them so far. "I'm surprised that you're all friends."

"Friends?" He's Dead objected, and he spat tobacco juice into the sink. "Not with the Laser. I hate his guts."

"But you admire my mind," Luke taunted.

Leon, the Reverend, shook his head in admiration. "Laser, I hear you were the only Steeler who had the whole playbook memorized, offense and defense."

He's Dead snorted. "He had to do something with all that time he spent sittin' on the bench."

"Who spent a whole season on crutches for a lousy bone spur?" Luke challenged immediately. "Listen, I was the one who ended up lying on the Astroturf and looking up at the clouds, not you. What's got you bugged after all these years?"

He's Dead shrugged. "I haven't got any outlets for my violent nature anymore, so I channel it into hatred. It saves wear and tear on the walls of my bedroom. After I retired, I used to punch a lot of walls," he explained to Grace.

"With his head," Blood added languidly, lighting a cigarette.

He's Dead splashed some beer on Blood's shirt to shut him up.

Grace watched and listened and tried to stay out of the way of flying liquids. The safest place was to stand right inside Luke's arms as he leaned against the kitchen counter to laugh and joke with his friends. She was too afraid to move away from him. He's Dead made continual references to her legs and smacked his lips if she got too close, and Blood looked so much like a glowering gargoyle that Grace shrank into Luke each time the big tackle came to the cooler for another beer. All the while, the music *wh-whammed* in the next room and the swinging door thudded open and closed as a gaggle of guests came in or out for more refreshments. One young woman, elegantly beautiful in siren-red shorts—shorts in February, no less—came dancing in to the beat of the music and grabbed the man named Leon by his belt. Dancing wordlessly, she led him out into the party and they disappeared, never to be seen again. The men in the kitchen all cheered, Luke included.

Before long Gizmo Montgomery, the host, came loping back into the kitchen. He got a slap on his behind in greeting from Blood, and he responded by punching his friend in the shoulder, a slamming blow that would have sent a lesser man flying. Blood barely moved at the contact.

Gizmo was the life of the party. "How you guys doin' back here? You gettin' enough to drink? Findin' any nice ladies? My sister's here, Blood, you gonna say hello?"

"Maybe," Blood said, not getting excited.

"And you, Laser? How you been, buddy? You gonna bring me one of those fancy cars you've been promisin'?"

"Sure," Luke said easily. "You want one or not?"

Gizmo winked. "You let me check with my old lady first. See if we've got the lettuce to pay you. Amazin' Grace, how you doin', honey? Somebody get you a beer yet?"

"I'm fine, thank you," Grace said quickly.

"You're waitin' for the entertainment, I can see. Hey, fellas!" Gizmo said, raising his voice. "I got *films* to show you later."

The men cheered and whistled.

"Football films," Gizmo corrected, and they all promptly booed. Gizmo objected, "Hey, hey, none of that. Once I knew the Laser was in town, I put together a montage of his greatest moments."

"Mon-*tage,*" He's Dead repeated, scoffing at the fancy word.

Gizmo ignored him and pointed a finger at Grace's nose. "Hey, Amazin', you'd like you see the Laser in action, wouldn'tcha?"

Blood observed, "I think she already has, my man."

Grace attempted to ignore the lewd implication. "I'd like to see some football film, as a matter of fact. It might be interesting."

"Hold it," Luke urged quietly, tugging Grace close once again with a smile. "He's not talking about my greatest moments exactly. Giz videotaped every professional football game since the beginning of time, and he's always putting together clips of the worst possible accidents—"

"Accidents?" He's Dead hooted. "Laser, those were accidents for *you,* but when I hit you on the field of battle, it was *heaven,* man, heaven! I want to see you eat the dirt!"

Luke groaned. "Can I skip this?"

"Let's go!" Gizmo shouted. "Down to the screening room, ladies and gents. This way. Let's see some *action!*"

Grace couldn't have hung back if she'd wanted to. The men all moved as one, and the bulldozing effect of professional football players all traveling in the same direction was an awesome force. Luke pushed her ahead of them like a quivering leaf before floodwaters.

The "screening room" was actually a large portion of Gizmo's basement that had been furnished with La-Z-Boy recliners and a beer keg. The walls were decorated with blown-up photographs of football players in various states of agony. An oversize television screen commanded one whole wall, and gigantic speakers flanked it. The rug was grasslike, and Grace caught her shoe on it and stumbled. Astroturf indoors? Surely not! Yes, there was a fifty-yard line painted in a white stripe right down the middle.

Gizmo strode across the green expanse to the television console, shoved a videotape into a slot, and pressed some buttons. The revelers crowded into the room behind him, bringing along the noise from upstairs. Someone splashed more beer on someone else. A woman squealed as one of the football players dragged her down with him into one of the reclining chairs in a tangle of long arms and legs. Shouts of laughter, a college fight song, and the drumming of fists on the side of the keg were all amplified by the closed-in room. Luke's arms wrapped protectively around Grace from behind, and she was thankful. He leaned against the back wall of the room, shunning the recliners, which filled up quickly anyway. The room was crowded in no time.

"Hit the lights!" Gizmo shouted, and in a split second the room was plunged into darkness. A picture blazed onto the television screen. It showed sunshine glaring down on a football field with a federal regulations warning indicating that to tape the following material for unauthorized use was illegal. The men in the recliners jeered at the message and threw more beer into the air.

Above the hubbub, Gizmo shouted, "Now, tonight's show opens with some clips of the dee-lightful Detroit Lions! Let's show a little respect, huh?" Then he ducked as a beer can came soaring at him.

Grace didn't understand exactly what she was looking at. All football teams and games looked alike to her. Some players wore white shirts and some wore dark ones, and they took turns trying to run past the goalposts with the ball. From the angle of the camera, she had trouble following who had the ball during the film clips that raced by the screen. That didn't seem to matter. The players around her howled when a lineman made a mistake, or cheered when the quarterback slipped and fell down. They didn't necessarily care who had the ball, but watched and reacted to the other action on the field, thumping each other's heads in delight when a tackle was made. Apparently, there was much more to football than Grace had realized.

And then Gizmo shouted, "Now, take a look at this! Why, I'll be horsewhipped: It's those pansy Pittsburgh Steelers!"

Booing erupted in the room, and somebody whacked Luke across the shoulder. He ducked, shielding Grace from the blow, but he was laughing with the rest of them.

The football jerseys were black and gold on one team and blue on the other.

"That's him, folks," Gizmo bellowed. "The wimpiest wide receiver, number eighty-one, Luke the Laser! Check him out! Let's see the man run!"

Grace found a shirt with the number eighty-one. Yes, she recognized Luke even with those outsize shoulder pads that made his hips look trim and cute and his legs long, graceful, and impossibly delicate. He was at the top of the screen, while the rest of the team collected on the line of scrimmage. He didn't crouch down into the three-point stance the way the other players did, but waited until the ball was snapped and then bolted out into enemy territory. The quarterback took six steps back, looked for Luke, and fired the ball straight at him. Luke caught the ball, tucked it into his side, and turned for the goal line. He ran beautifully— but only about four steps. Then somebody in a blue shirt came out of nowhere and slammed into him with the force of a speeding freight train. They crashed to the ground together with a tremendous concussion. The crowd cheered.

Then came another clip appearing on the screen and another, all showing pretty much the same action. Luke caught the football each time, ran a few steps, and was again tackled and hurled painfully into the turf. Grace winced with every fall, and she heard herself gasp once.

"This is my favorite," Gizmo shouted. "Take a look. Fourth down and fifteen yards to go. It's a pressure situation. Look at the clock. Ten seconds to the half. They've got to score this time! Ball is snapped. Bradshaw fades back, looks for his receiver. Where the hell is Lazurnovich, folks?"

Grace watched. The camera shifted, and Luke came tearing out of a scramble of blue shirts. The ball soared right for him, but too high. The action switched to slow motion as Luke went leaping up to make the catch. It was beautiful to watch, for he just went higher and higher until the ball came smoothly into his hands. Only he never made it back to earth, it seemed.

"It's the free safety coming to cream the Laser!" Gizmo screamed.

Another player—Grace guessed immediately that it was He's Dead Jim McCoy—came up from underneath and caught Luke just above his knees. In midair, Luke did a slow-motion somersault, going helplessly end over end. Another blue-shirted player slammed him in the ribs as he started downward, and the force propelled Luke up and backward even more.

"He's goin' into orbit!" Gizmo shouted. "The man's feet never touch the ground! Unbelievable!"

Yet another player, his arm outstretched, hit Luke across the head. For an awful moment, Grace thought his head had been ripped off by the blow. But it was only his helmet— sent sailing off screen. Luke arched into another impossible somersault. The slow motion made the action agonizing. Grace covered her mouth with both her hands to keep from crying out. The human body wasn't capable of withstanding the kind of impact he was about to endure.

Luke's second somersault went only halfway. He hit the ground with one shoulder first, bounced, and crashed to the earth with such force that the whole room shouted *"Oh!"* in unison. Grace could feel Luke go tight behind her as he watched and remembered the crash.

"But he never drops the ball!" Gizmo shouted excitedly. "And watch this! It just kills me! He gets up! He actually *gets up!* He doesn't know where he is, folks, but he's on his feet!"

On screen, Luke rolled neatly and somehow managed to get upright. He was indeed standing. He didn't budge, though. He stood very still while the rest of the players milled around. Without his helmet, it was easy to see that Luke couldn't focus his eyes. His dark, curling hair ruffled in the breeze. The other players walked away. The referee came and pried the ball out of his hands, but still Luke didn't move.

"He's *out!*" said He's Dead over the erupting howls of laughter. "Ever see a man with the Tweety birds inside his head? There he is! The man was unconscious on his feet!"

The camera stayed with Luke until another player—Grace presumed it was He's Dead—came up and waved his hand in front of Luke's face. No response. The rest of the people in the room were dying with laughter, and Grace was stunned. How could they be so amused by such violence?

The camera cut away finally to show two more shots of Luke getting rammed into semiconsciousness by other players. Each was so horrible that Grace couldn't speak, couldn't move. She felt isolated, even though Luke's arm remained snug around her and the room was packed with shouting people. She felt as though she were the only one who didn't understand, who didn't *want* to understand. Even Luke was enjoying himself. Grace felt sick.

Then the television screen stopped tormenting Luke and moved on to another player, Blood. But since Blood wasn't a man who caught the ball and didn't attract the tackles of other players, those film clips mostly illustrated his funny mistakes. The party crowd roared with laughter. Grace was horribly fascinated by the monstrous physical punishment that was displayed on the screen.

And the party had taken on the flavor of a Roman coliseum, with shouts of delight filling the air after each tremendous concussion. To Grace, it was decadent and shocking. She hadn't imagined such horrors could be anyone's idea of fun.

Abruptly, the lights came on and Gizmo got up to make another speech. Someone near the screen began to shout, "No way! Take a hike, Montomery! Take a hike!"

The crowd took up the chant, getting rowdy. Someone hurled a can of beer at Gizmo, who didn't duck in time. The beer splashed all over him, soaking his hair and his shirt. He reacted promptly, firing his own can back at his attacker. The fight was on. Suddenly the air was full of soaring beer cans, sloshing everyone.

Luke groaned comically. "Oh, no," he said, and he started to push Grace toward the door. He laughed a little, watching the action over his shoulder as he said to her, "You don't want to see this, Princess. Once they get started, nobody's safe."

Grace faltered. She wasn't sure why. It was a little like watching huge animals tear each other's throat out, she supposed—horribly fascinating.

"C'mon, Laser! Hit me, hit me!"

Out of nowhere, a can whizzed past Luke's ear and hit the wall, practically exploding with the force and drenching Luke in the process. He ducked just in time to avoid the ricocheting can. A shout of delight erupted from behind them, and a flurry of cans crashed against the nearby wall. A woman screamed. Everyone else was laughing.

And then a lone can soared into the air and zoomed directly at Grace. Without thinking, she put out her hands to stop it. Beer splattered in every direction, but primarily all over the front of her dress.

Someone yelled, "Score!"

"Quick," Luke urged, laughing with the others. "Get out before we've got to swim!"

Grace turned to go, but at the last instant, yet another aluminium can arched at her from across the room. It struck her just above the breastbone, sending a spray of beer splashing down her body, soaking her to the skin.

"Score!" Luke shouted with the rest, howling with laughter.

Amid the hilarity, Grace swung on Luke, glaring at him.

"It's just a game," he shouted, lifting his hands in a classically innocent shrug. "It's not real, for crying out loud!"

By now Grace was in a furious, shaken rage. "How could you? What do you think *I* feel? You're all crazy!"

"No, we're not," Luke roared, his eyes alight with laughter and probably too much beer. He grabbed her close to him and said, "It's just a game, that's all. It's funny!"

"It is *not* funny!" Grace yelled, tearing herself free. She lunged breathlessly for the door and escaped the mob. The stairwell was cool and lighted by a single bare lightbulb. Luke was just a step behind, thudding up the stairs.

"Hey!" he called after her as Grace charged upward. "Princess! Wait a mintue!"

She turned, her face white with shock and anger. Trembling, she insisted, "I will not wait another minute. This place is horrible! These people are horrible! They frighten me!"

Luke halted three steps below her, his hand on the railing. Shaking his head in amusement, he said, "Nobody's going to hurt you. It's just a little beer—it doesn't even stain anything. It's a good time."

"For jungle beasts this might be a good time," Grace retorted. "For civilized human beings it's—it's—well, I can't even think of anything disgusting enough to compare this party to!"

Behind Luke, the basement door opened again. It was He's Dead Jim McCoy, looking huge. He had a smirk on his face, and with one look up at Grace and back down at Luke, he had the whole scenario figured out. He folded his arms across his chest and said, "Whatsamatter, Laser? You letting your old lady push you around?"

Luke didn't answer right away. Silent, he looked up at Grace, his eyes dark suddenly. He didn't smile.

Grace met his look with an angry one of her own. Distinctly, she said, "I'm ready to go now."

"Go?" He's Dead objected. "You can't leave yet. The party's just gettin' started."

Luke still didn't respond.

Grace flushed abruptly. The least a gentleman could do was speak up for a lady in this kind of situation! But Luke remained resentfully silent, and that made Grace even angrier. How had she ever thought he was attractive? She snapped, "Take me back to the hotel now, please."

He's Dead gave a laugh. In a squeaky voice, he mimicked, "'Take me back now, honey.' C'mon, Laser, you gonna walk out on us?"

"No," Luke said dangerously.

"I want to go," Grace repeated, matching his tone.

"Then I'll call you a cab," Luke said.

Grace had never felt so furious in her whole life.

CHAPTER TEN

THE NEXT MORNING Grace had a nine-o'clock appointment at a Detroit television station, so she was awakened by her alarm clock at seven-thirty. Luke had not slept beside her. In fact, she hadn't heard him come back from Gizmo's party. Annoyed, exasperated, and finally furious with the situation in which she found herself, Grace took a very hot shower. She dressed, repacked her suitcases and left them on her bed, and then prepared to leave the suite to have breakfast in a public restaurant for once.

When she opened the bedroom door, with coat and attaché case in hand, she was arrested by the sight that greeted her eyes. Luke had indeed returned from the party, although he had wisely chosen not to join Grace in the bedroom. He had also shunned the couch, for its meager length could never accommodate a man of his size. He had taken a few of the cushions, however, and was wrapped in a blanket on the floor. He was sound asleep, fully dressed.

Grace stood over his body and glared down at him. A quick kick in his stomach, and she could be out in the hallway before Luke ever knew what hit him.

No, no, she chided herself, that would be stooping to his level. And what an incredibly low level that was!

He gave a long snuffle and then a real snore. For once, he looked terrible. His hair was a mess, and standing over his inert frame, Grace could smell the reek of cigarettes and stale beer. Apparently, beer throwing was an integral part of a football player's repertoire of skills. Luke had obviously received his share of the dousings. Grace wrinkled her nose in distaste. The man was positively a slob.

Head high, she made a swift about-face and stalked toward the door. She cut quickly around the couch, heading out for breakfast and a quiet, sensible review of her own thoughts. She stumbled to a stop, however, in astonishment.

There was a young woman sleeping on the couch. She was blond and pretty and about twenty-one, and she was wearing a football jersey. A pair of bright green platform shoes had been left on the floor. Unconsciously, Grace took a step toward the couch, imagining for one whirlwind of a moment that this was a mirage.

Surely he couldn't have brought a girl back with him! How impossibly disgusting! How could one man be so loathsome? So nauseating? So unfeelingly horrible?

Grace turned around, took three quick strides, and kicked Luke right in the kidneys. He sucked in a breath, groaned, and lay still again. In outrage, Grace stormed for the door. He couldn't even give a satisfactory scream of agony!

She rode the elevator down to the lobby in a fury. Muttering to herself, she stomped through the lobby and shoved her way out onto the street. She walked the whole way to the television station in a rage.

Therefore, naturally, the television interview went badly. Grace looked as if she'd walked through a wind tunnel, and the makeup artist kept patting powder on her face during the commercial breaks, asking if she was perhaps nervous or upset about something. Grace couldn't very well say that she, Dear Ms. Barrett, had become emotionally involved with a Neanderthal boor, but she was tempted to confide in someone—anyone!—about how stupid she had been.

After the program, she had to hail a cab and run across town to a local bookstore for a lunchtime autograph session. By two o'clock, she was on her way back to the hotel. She wondered what she was going to discover there. Would Luke play it smart and disappear from her life entirely? Or was he going to hang around and plead pitifully for forgiveness? And what exactly was the best way to make him grovel?

When her cab deposited her in front of the hotel, however, Grace had to think fast. Luke's Jaguar was parked out front. The trunk was open, and her own suitcases stood on the sidewalk. A pair of bellhops looked on nervously. The hood of the long car was also open, and Luke was busy underneath it.

Dear Ms. Barrett,

While enrolled in a handgun class at a local firing range, I found myself falling in love with a man who is not a member of my socio-economic station in life. I have learned to overlook his shortcomings in private, but now that our relationship has come in 'off the range,' so to speak, I find myself frequently annoyed by his quick-trigger temper, lewd jokes, and degrading remarks. I have followed your advice and tried guiding him into more acceptable behavior, but without much success. Now what? I'm quite attached to him and would be so disappointed if I had to put a bullet in our relationship and end the suffering.

—Hair Trigger in Harrisburg

Dear Hair,

Is Ann Landers on vacation? Why are you dear readers asking me such questions? If you insist on extracting my opinion, I suggest either that you shoot him or yourself. Why suffer the indignity? Even love must have limits.

Luke must have seen part of her coat as Grace stood on the opposite side of the open hood. He finished with his adjusting first, however, and straightened to face her. He was cleaning off his hands on a less than immaculate rag. Dressed in his jeans and yellow sweater again, he looked a little healthier than he had while lying zonked on the floor in a blanket, but not by much. He had a gray blotch just above each cheekbone and a bleary squint to his eyes, as though he was nursing an incredible headache. He didn't crack a smile.

Grace met his baleful stare with an imperiously haughty look. "Well, at least you're vertical."

Luke did not retort. He slammed the hood down.

Grace blinked politely. "Are you going somewhere?"

Luke walked the length of the Jaguar and threw his rag into the trunk. He reached for her first suitcase. "Yes."

"With my luggage?" Grace asked, hurrying to the rear of the car. "Just where do you think you're going?"

"St. Louis," he said distinctly, stowing the suitcases inside the car. "You have an interview there tomorrow night at six-thirty. There are no trains between here and there. Get in."

Grace held her ground, although she had an awful feeling that she was losing the battle before it got started. She repeated, "Get in?"

Luke slammed down the trunk, but couldn't stop his own wince of pain. He must have a doozy of a headache. He controlled himself, however, and said shortly, "You heard me."

Grace assumed her straightest, most regal posture, and lifted her nose a full inch higher. "If I do choose to obey your command, you can rest assured that it is not because of any absurd emotion that you might imagine I am feeling for you."

"Of course not," Luke said, matching her cold hauteur with a sneering arrogance of his own. "I would never imagine that you are capable of the least bit of feeling, Dear Ms. Barrett. Now, get in the car."

"I have one question."

"One?" Luke asked, eyeing her with a clear promise of violence in his eyes. "Just one?"

Nodding once, Grace said, "Just one, and then I would

prefer to forget the past forty-eight hours, if you please."

"Suits me," said Luke. "Shoot."

"All right," Grace replied coolly. "Who was she?"

He didn't ask her to clarify the question. Luke knew precisely about whom Grace was asking. He came around the side of the car, oblivious to the two bellhops who hastily scrambled out of his way, and he opened the passenger door for her. As she was about to get in, pausing before him with delicately lifted eyebrows, he said composedly, "To tell you the truth, I don't know who she was."

That was that, unfortunately. Grace swallowed the next most obvious question in view of her promise to ask just one, and she simply got into the Jaguar and waited calmly while Luke went around the front. He stopped. With annoyance, he snatched a parking ticket out from under the windshield wiper. Crumpling it into his pocket, he snapped open the car door and got in on his side. He slammed the door, reached for the ignition, and revved the car's engine. Then he put his hand under the seat, groped, and came up with his headphones. He plugged them into his ears, switched on his music, and did not speak for the next five hours.

So Grace fumed. She made a pretense of working, for Lucy had sent a packet of letters for Dear Ms. Barrett to answer, and with her lapboard to provide a hard surface, Grace used her Cross pen and dusty-rose notepaper to respond to her inquisitive readers. Later she would have to rewrite the entire batch, for she could not concentrate.

She was crazy, she told herself. She had just passed up a perfect opportunity to suggest that Luke travel to a much warmer place in a hand basket, and she'd backed down and actually gotten into the car with him again. Why? Why were they staying together? Why hadn't he just gone home? Why didn't she have enough pride to dump him and go on the tour alone?

Perhaps it was pride that made her stick with him. It had become a sort of contest. Grace wanted to prove that she could be cooler and calmer than Luke. The only trouble was that he was pretty darn cool, too.

Then, of course, there was Dear Ms. Barrett's voice in

the back of her head, saying with Mother's haughtiest in-
tonation, "Grace, this man is not suitable. Perhaps you
haven't realized it yet, but he hails from a completely different world. With your breeding and upbringing, and his
total lack of either one, this relationship is doomed."

Another part of Grace was whispering a different message, however. Luke was a tough guy—not just rough around
the edges, but strong enough to stand up to her. Few men
could boast that they had defied Grace Barrett and won.
That alone set Luke apart from Kip and the other men around
the fringes of her life. The more Grace thought about it, the
more she realized that Luke was demonstrating classic passive resistance. He wasn't going to be the one to decide
they should go their separate ways! This had become a
challenge, and neither of them was going to back down or
give an inch. It was a standoff.

It made her a little sad. They were just too different, that
was all. Their two worlds were so dramatically separate that
they couldn't possibly weave them together into one lifestyle. After the book tour, she was not going to see him
again. Grace swallowed hard when that thought crossed her
mind. And she was strangely sorry.

Luke drove and listened to his headphones. He didn't
try to make conversation, and Grace decided that part of
the reason was that he was feeling terrible from his celebration of the night before. Not once on the long drive to
St. Louis did he stop for his usual two-hour feeding. He
must be really hung over if he wasn't eating.

Darkness came, and Grace began to get hungry and tired.
She didn't dare break the silence first. That would show
who was weaker. She dozed off for a short time, and then
the car told her they were close to their destination with the
changing of gears and the stop-starting at traffic signals.
But when she opened her eyes and looked around, she knew
they weren't in St. Louis.

She sat up abruptly. There wasn't a building in sight,
just snowy fields and fences. Finally, they passed a barn
and then a closed vegetable stand, dusted with snowflakes.
Luke didn't explain, but pulled the car through a wide farm

gate and then around a driveway where two pickup trucks and a battered station wagon were parked. There stood a farmhouse, all the lights burning like a picture on a Christmas card. A collie sat on his haunches on the porch like a lookout. The dog barked at the car's approach.

Grace couldn't stand it any longer. She turned to Luke. "Where are we?"

Luke took his headphones off. "Home."

"Home?"

He set the car's brake and shut off the engine. "Yeah. We'll stay here tonight. Get your coat. It's cold."

The dog leaped feebly off the porch and walked to the car, barking. Grace hesitated to get out, for the beast sounded ferocious. His head was white, though, and he had the big-bellied, thin-legged look of an elderly dog. When Luke got out of the car, the collie stopped barking and began to wag his plumed tail.

Luke cuffed the dog affectionately on his way to the trunk. Then the farmhouse door opened and the golden light from inside spilled out onto the porch.

"Luke? That you?"

A big man in a flannel shirt and loose-fitting green work trousers stood silhouetted in the doorway. He didn't step over the threshold, and when Grace followed Luke up the wooden steps, she saw that the man was in his stocking feet, having left his shoes somewhere in the house.

Luke stood back to let Grace go through the door first. "Pop," he said, "meet Grace Barrett. Princess, this is my father, Peter Lazurnovich."

Although Peter was shorter and stouter, and had a shock of thick white hair instead of curly brown, father and son were very alike. Peter's eyes were just as blue, his smile just as crookedly pleasant, and his hand just as warm and firm as Luke's. He clasped Grace hard, drawing her into the warmth of the house. "How-do, Miss Barrett. Glad you could come stay with us."

"Th-thank you," Grace said, stepping over a tiger-striped cat that lay on the circular rag rug underfoot. From Peter Lazurnovich's manner, she guessed that she and Luke were expected. Luke must have called his parents before they left Detroit.

Luke dropped the luggage on the oak floor and turned to his father with a grin. The men met each other's sparkling eyes and shook hands, a grip that immediately turned into an affectionate wrestling match. Luke gave up first, crying out with pretended agony when his father twisted his arm hard.

A shout came from somewhere in the house, a male bellow of alertness. Heavy footsteps followed, and then suddenly the small entry hall was crowded with huge men. From their blue-eyed looks and easy manners, Grace knew immediately that she was being confronted by Luke's brothers. The dog began to bark again with excitement.

No one bothered to make formal introductions. The first Lazurnovich brother pumped her hand and said his name was Mark. He was not much taller than Grace and whip-thin. Then came Matt and John, both just as tall as Luke, but much heavier. They all hugged their brother Luke or punched him playfully amid shouts of welcome.

Then came a gaggle of children, some wild and excited, others hanging timidly around their fathers' legs and peeping up at Luke with round eyes. Behind the kids were the women, undoubtedly the Lazurnovich wives, all different shapes and sizes, but wearing uniformly big smiles of welcome. Marie, Jackie, and Gwen. Gwen was pregnant, and Jackie was a giantess, tall and lanky. Marie had curly blond hair and an apron that read: I'D RATHER BE ANYWHERE BUT THIS KITCHEN.

It was Marie who drew off Grace's coat and led her back along the hall to escape the hullabaloo. "We were so surprised to hear from Luke! Mamma called us all over for supper tonight. We couldn't wait to see him! It's been since Thanksgiving! Have you been together long? Isn't he sweet?"

Grace kept up her smile and tried to answer, although her responses didn't seem important, and then they arrived in a kitchen the size of a small restaurant. Grace took a deep breath to inhale the luxurious mixture of cooking smells, for a fragrant cloud hung in the oven-warmed room. Pots were roiling with steam on the stove; a pan of fresh-baked rolls stood glistening on the sideboard. She also saw a pitcher of milk, a plate of butter, an enormous slab of ham, crocks and casseroles and baskets and bottles. One look, and Grace was starving.

A woman turned from the refrigerator, her hands rubbing together inside her apron. She was stocky, and not tall as Grace would have expected of Luke's mother. She wore a dress, a cotton shirtwaist with a cardigan sweater over it, the sleeves pushed Luke-style above her elbows. Her hair was reddish-brown and her eyes were dark like deep running waters and just as cold. She looked directly at Grace and didn't smile. Grace knew then exactly where Luke got his pride and self-confidence.

"Mamma," said Marie at Grace's shoulder, "this is Luke's friend, Grace Barrett. They just got here."

"I heard," said Luke's mother, crossing the linoleum floor. "I'm not deaf yet. Hello, miss. Luke says you're a writer."

Grace shook hands with Mrs. Lazurnovich and wasn't surprised by the strength in the other woman's grip. One look at Mrs. Lazurnovich's eyes told Grace precisely where she stood—and that position was mighty low. This greeting was worse than a total rejection. Mrs. Lazurnovich wasn't going to thaw until Grace proved herself worthy of the family's company. Without completely understanding why she suddenly felt so intimidated, Grace said, "Yes, ma'am."

"Hmph," Mrs. Lazurnovich replied, eyeing Grace's slim figure and stylish skirt and blouse with a blank look that neither approved or disapproved. "Marie, go check those potatoes."

Then the crowd surged into the kitchen, which suddenly seemed very small with the noisy family milling around. Mrs. Lazurnovich turned away from Grace without another word. Grace felt like a teenager again—one who'd just been rejected by the most popular kid in class.

Mrs. Lazurnovich's face lit up when she saw Luke, though, and she hurried into his arms. With a laugh, he hugged her hard, picking her up off the floor. The rest of the family crowded around, particularly the children, who realized that once Grandma Lazurnovich gave her approval, this big uncle must be okay after all.

"Hey, hey," called Mark when the reunion was complete. "What about dinner? We've been hungry for hours!"

Mrs. Lazurnovich took charge, clapping her hands like a kindergarten teacher and issuing commands. "You boys clear out of here and get the chairs set around. Girls, you get this food out on the table. Jackie, check those biscuits in the oven, and then, if the kids have eaten already, you send 'em down to watch TV while we have our supper. Luke, you come with me. I'll see you and this girl to your rooms, and you can wash up."

Everybody obeyed with alacrity. Grace, having been referred to as "this girl," understood her position immediately. She was an outsider and was unapproved by the family as yet. She meekly followed Luke and his mother back down the hallway to the entryway. Luke kept his arm across Mrs. Lazurnovich's shoulders, and he laughed and teased her about her auburn hair, which was a new color, Grace guessed, by the snippets of conversation that she could hear.

Luke carried their luggage upstairs, and Mrs. Lazurnovich directed him down the narrow hallway. "You sleep down there in your brother's room tonight, hear? Matt's boy Tom is staying in there, too. This girl can sleep up in your old room by herself."

"What's the matter, Mamma?" Luke asked, although he was already heading down the hall in the direction she ordered him. "You think there's gonna be hanky-panky tonight?"

"Not under my roof!" his mother retorted. "I sleep like a cat, remember, so don't you try sneakin' up and down the hall later! This way, miss. There's a bathroom here, and you take this room. Nothing fancy, but the bed's comfortable. We're havin' supper in a few minutes, so don't dawdle."

"Yes, ma'am," Grace said meekly as she squeezed past her hostess and bolted into the bedroom as quickly as possible.

Dear Ms. Barrett,

*My mother-in-law hates me. I'm not good enough
for her son, and from the way she acts, you'd think
I smell as if I've spent too much time in the hog pens.
She doesn't insult me, exactly. She ignores me. Is it
too much to ask for a little respect?*

—Bugged in Bismarck

Dear Bis,

*It has been my observation that mothers-in-law
are frequently displeased with their sons' choices in
spouses. You have two courses of action: Ignore her
back and be thankful she's not insisting that you spend
all your time with the hogs; or be as sweet and helpful
and polite as you possibly can—really ham it up, if
you know what I mean. Ms. Barrett hesitates to suggest the third and most obvious option, which is to
have a baby. She'll love you for that!*

It was not possible to have a baby in the next half hour,
and Grace knew she couldn't risk ignoring Mamma Lazurnovich. She was going to have to make the best of it, and
without Luke's help. It looked as if he were letting her sink
or swim.

He didn't even sit with her at dinner. Grace was ordered
into the chair at the end of the table on Peter's right. Mark
Lazurnovich sat beside her, and Marie was across the table.
Luke sat down near his mother and beside Gwen. As they
all took their places at the table Grace watched as pregnant
Gwen took Luke's hand and slid it up under her sweater so
he could feel her big belly. They laughed together when the
baby kicked, and Grace looked away quickly, feeling annoyed. And then abandoned.

Peter Lazurnovich called attention, folded his hands, and
began to say a prayer. His words were not a chanted reci-
tation, but a chatty kind of thank-you to God that also let
Him know how the family was getting along lately. Smiling,
Grace peeked; she looked around the table to see all four

of the brothers with their elbows on the table and their hands folded like well-mannered schoolboys, eyes closed. It was an amusing sight—for between them, the brothers and their father probably weighed nearly half a ton. But it was also a little touching, and abruptly Grace felt like even more of an outsider. When Mr. Lazurnovich finally said "Amen," all the Lazurnovichs crossed themselves and prepared to eat.

Conversations broke out immediately, everyone asking or answering questions all at once while the steaming dishes and laden platters were passed up and down the long, crowded table. Mark attuned himself to Grace, suggesting she try this salad that his wife had made or that fancy potato because it was his grandmother's recipe and Luke's favorite, and did she come from a farm herself? No, Grace told him carefully that she didn't, but she'd taken a trip to one once with her third-grade class. Mark laughed easily, and in just a few minutes he was confident enough with Grace to start teasing her a little. He called his father in on the conversation, and soon Grace found herself telling them about her own grandmother Barrett and the special cinnamon crown rolls that appeared at the Barrett holiday table.

Gradually, the family began to eat, and the many conversations turned into just one. Luke was the star, of course. He was asked about his business, and Grace was interested to learn that he was looking to expand and was hunting for a new location. He told his father about a fancy car that had come into his hands with a generator problem, and Peter asked some technical questions. They talked cars for a while, then Mrs. Lazurnovich interrupted with a series of questions about Luke's business affairs, until she was interrupted in turn by Gwen, who wanted to know all about Luke's trip with Grace.

"Oh," Luke said casually, without glancing toward Grace's end of the table, "we just happened to be traveling in the same direction, that's all. Did I tell you that Sikorsky fellow from St. Louis wants to be my partner? He's called me twice since Christmas."

"Sikorsky!" Mark objected. "He's afraid of your competition. You going to join forces with a dealer, Luke? I thought you liked running your own shop."

Luke shrugged and passed the butter to his mother. "It'd be nice to be able to leave somebody else in charge once in a while. I've got an assistant who's not bad. I have to call him every day that I'm not there, though, just to keep him from panicking. I need a change. Everybody needs one of those now and then. Is there pie for dessert?"

As the marathon dinner continued, no one asked Grace what her business was. Apparently, prying into her life was not considered polite in this family circle. Coffee came when Grace thought her stomach would burst from all the savory dishes, and then rhubarb-strawberry pie appeared, her favorite.

"I've kept these in the freezer," Mrs. Lazurnovich said as she cut into the first one. "We didn't eat 'em all at Christmas this year."

"Don't give us that story," Mark retorted cheerfully. "You kept a few back for Luke. You're still spoiling him."

"I spoiled you worse than all of the rest put together," she shot back, passing Mark an enormous piece of pie.

Grace had eaten too much and she was very drowsy after finishing her pie. She listened as the family tipped their chairs back to talk some more. It was nice to sit and hear this tightly knit midwestern family trade bits of information. Mark, the lively one, was an accountant, and his wife, Gwen, was managing a bookstore until their baby arrived. It was to be their first child, and they were delighted and obviously still in the bloom of love. Silent and thoughtful Matt worked as a clerk in a feed store, and his wife, Marie, full of spirit and good humor, stayed home with their young children. John, the biggest of all the brothers and perhaps the one who had a coarse joke or two ready for when the men had a moment alone together, was a construction worker and was temporarily unemployed. Jackie, his wife, was a schoolteacher, and kept the family out of the unemployment line—a practice still considered a disgrace by the Lazurnovich men. John was acting as temporary house-husband, and there were many jokes aimed at his laundry skills.

There was nothing sophisticated or affected about the Lazurnovich clan, Grace decided. They were honest and happy people who delighted in keeping the family close and strong. She thought of her own family, often cynical and rarely together anymore, and she felt a tug of remorse.

Eventually, the men got some cans of beer and went downstairs to the television, while Grace helped the women clear the table. The kitchen was a terrific mess, reflecting the quantity and variety of the meal they'd just enjoyed. It was nearly eleven o'clock before everything was put right again. By that time, Grace was practically asleep on her feet.

Jackie and Marie rounded up their children—there must have been eight between them—and started the task of finding coats and hats and mittens for all. Gwen dragged the men away from a televised basketball game. After a half hour of good-byes and when-we-see-you-agains, Luke's brothers took their families to their own nearby homes.

When they had left, and Luke came back into the foyer from helping pack the children into the station wagon, he brushed the snow from his sweater and spoke to Grace for the first time all evening.

"You ought to go to bed," he said. "You must be bored, and you look tired."

"I'm not bored," Grace said, and she couldn't stop herself from reaching to dust a few snowflakes from his hair. She retreated a quick half step, uncertain of his reaction to her familiarity. "I—I'm sorry I look tired."

Luke didn't move. His father, who was in the dining room, called to Mrs. Lazurnovich, "Where's my pipe, Faith?" and she shouted from the kitchen, "Don't you light that thing up in this house tonight, Peter Lazurnovich. Go out to the porch!"

So, with Luke's parents affectionately squabbling in the distance and the purring cat sliding around their legs for attention, the half-light created by a lamp in the upstairs hall and the still heavy fragrances of ham and pie and coffee in the air, the moment was suddenly intimate between Luke and Grace. The angry tension melted away, to be replaced by a different kind of tension. Suddenly, Grace longed to walk into Luke's arms. She wanted to share the security of his family, the warmth of this evening, and the closeness she swiftly needed. But she was afraid of what had happened between them since the day before. Things weren't easy and funny and quick with Luke anymore.

He touched her on her cheek with his fingertips and tipped her face to the slanting light. His blue eyes had a kind of smoldering look, no longer hostile. Quietly he corrected himself, saying, "You look lovely, Princess."

Grace didn't smile. She didn't trust her mouth not to quiver. Suddenly, her emotions were bubbling inside like a caldron of volatile elements. Although there was a tremor in her voice, she began urgently, "Luke . . ."

He must have seen that she couldn't say what was on her mind. He put out his hand, offering her his strength, and Grace slipped hers into it. They clasped hands then, entwining their fingers until the fit was snug and communicative, and they met each other's eyes for a long moment, holding their breaths. Whatever Luke saw in her stinging gaze caused him to slide his other arm around her waist. As if hypnotized, he pulled her against him. She melted into Luke's body, wrapping her arms around his neck naturally, gratefully. With a caress of his fingertips, he guided her mouth higher and finally to his. Then, leaning against the newel at the bottom of the stairs, they were kissing, very softly, very gently.

There was no fever in Grace's veins this time, no sexual tide that obliterated her logic and reasoning. But her heart ker-whammed once and stopped, it seemed, suspended by the almost painful realization that shot into the unguarded part of her mind like an invading arrow. With Luke shyly tracing the contour of her lips with his tongue, as if seeking some sign that all had been forgiven and their natural bond had been restored, Grace realized that she was in love with him. She had fallen in love with Luke the Laser in an astonishingly short time, and for more reasons than just his ability to make her weak and wobbly with desire. The realization ought to have startled her, but strangely it didn't.

She moved against him, perfecting the contact of their two bodies until her breasts were firmly pressed against his chest and she was warmly filling with liquid love. Luke's arm tightened, holding her inescapably in his longing embrace, his kiss deepening. Passion came in a slow, inexorable wave, filling Grace, weakening her body, heating her blood, squeezing a barely audible sigh from her tight chest. In her head, Luke's name repeated itself, time and again.

But there were footsteps in the hall, and Luke immediately loosened his hold. He let Grace slide away but held her eyes with his. In his suddenly shadowy blue gaze, Grace read surprise, perhaps bewilderment, just before the sparkle, the wicked gleam she hadn't seen in so long, returned. Luke didn't smile, though; he just held her hand very tightly.

His mother came into the light, with Luke's nine-year-old nephew in tow. "I think you know my feelings about this, Luke," Mrs. Lazurnovich said gruffly.

He snapped out of his reverie but pulled Grace close once more, to make room for traffic in the hall. "What?"

Mrs. Lazurnovich kept coming and did not stop beside them. She made the corner and started up the steps, dragging young Tom by his head so he wouldn't see the display of adult affection. "About your carryin' on. You're a grown man and know your own business, but in my house we go by my rules, you understand?"

Luke let out a sigh of exasperated good humor. "Yes, Mamma. I'll behave myself in your house. Good night, Princess. I'll see you in the morning," he told Grace.

"Good night, Luke." Even to her own ears, her voice had an unmistakably wistful tone.

CHAPTER ELEVEN

AT MIDMORNING GRACE found Luke in the barn with his father under the hood of a vintage pickup truck. The barn hadn't been used for anything other than a garage for decades, and there were no signs of animals, except for the collie. The dog announced Grace's arrival, and both men ducked out from under the hood and stood straight upon hearing the noise. The expression in Luke's eyes set off a glorious chain reaction in Grace's brain, like all the neon lights on Broadway suddenly blinking on one after the other. By the time she'd caught her breath, her head was empty except for pure delight. After a night of dreaming about Luke, she could finally lay eyes on the man again.

He came around the yawning hood of the truck toward her, obviously conscious that his hands were filthy. He didn't touch her anywhere except to kiss her mouth. "Hey," he said in soft greeting, "sleep all right?"

"Fine, yes," Grace said, aware that she was turning three shades of pink—with Luke's father watching, no less! Like an idiot, she tried to cover her fluctuating emotions with a weak observation. "You're up early."

"Always," Luke said with a grin. "I learned it young."

Abruptly realizing what his smile was doing to her insides, Grace turned to his father. "Good morning, Mr. Lazurnovich. Did I thank you for allowing me to stay last night?"

With a knowing smile, just like Luke's, on his wide mouth, Peter Lazurnovich waved off her polite words. "Don't get all formal, Gracie. Call me Pete. We're glad to have you with us. Don't let Luke's mamma make you think otherwise."

"Oh," Grace objected quickly, "Mrs. Lazurnovich has been most kind. I wouldn't dream of—"

Peter shook his head, cutting off her protest. "She's touchy where her boys are concerned, that's all. It'll take a while for her to warm up to you. Don't fret. She likes you already, I can tell."

Well, Mrs. Lazurnovich could have fooled Grace! Luke's mother had even driven off to do some shopping in town that morning so she could be spared sitting with her son's guest at the breakfast table. At least, Grace was sure that was her reason for leaving for the morning. She didn't mention her feelings to Luke and his father when the men accompanied her back to the house and had cups of coffee while Grace breakfasted on toast and juice. They talked for a while, and Grace found that Luke had inherited his sense of humor from his father. Peter Lazurnovich had a certain amount of manly charm, also.

Mrs. Lazurnovich did return for lunch, however, in time to shake Grace's hand coolly in farewell and say good-bye properly to Luke, complete with hugs and kisses and a CARE package of ham sandwiches and a Thermos of coffee for the road.

Then Grace shook hands with Luke's father, who winked broadly at her to soften the blow of his wife's poorly disguised dissatisfaction, and with obvious sincerity urged Grace to return sometime. At least she'd been a hit with one of Luke's parents, Grace thought ruefully.

Finally, Luke put Grace into the passenger seat of the

Jaguar once again and they set off for St. Louis. Alone together at last, they were silent for several miles. Grace let her mind wander over the memory of the last day, thinking of Luke's home, his family, and particularly his brothers.

Finally, a thought flashed into her mind, and she said it spontaneously. "Matthew, Mark, Luke, and John."

Luke nodded. "That's us. The Lazurnovich brothers. And somebody called the Steelers awesome."

"You're all huge," Grace agreed, glancing at Luke's profile with a small smile.

"Except for Mark. He's the shrimp, so he makes up for it in fast talk and angelic looks." Luke relaxed in his seat, getting comfortable as he drove. A moment later, he added, "When we were kids and got into trouble, the gospel according to Saint Mark was always 'I wasn't anywhere near them when it happened!'"

Grace laughed at his squeaky-voiced imitation of Mark and then asked, "What was the gospel according to Saint Luke?"

"I was never a saint," Luke corrected with a grin across at her. "And being the next to the youngest, I was never a ringleader, either. It was nice and safe being a middle child."

Quietly, Grace said, "Your family is very nice. Thank you."

"For what?"

"Taking me there. It was an unexpected highlight of my tour."

Luke looked over at her, perhaps measuring her words. "You're not sore because I didn't ask you first?" he said.

"I don't suppose I would have gone if you'd asked me," Grace replied honestly.

Luke nodded. "I knew that. You probably figured the Lazurnovich family didn't bother to wash up when they came in from the barn, and maybe wrung the necks of chickens just for the fun of it."

"I did not—" Grace began to object.

"No, no," Luke interrupted with a laugh. "Don't lie. You decided a long time ago, Dear Ms. Barrett, that I was a rude and crude dude. Why should my kinfolk be any different?"

Grace found that she was bristling automatically at his choice of words, taunting her with his inelegant speech. She said, "I'll admit that in the brief time we've known each other you haven't exactly demonstrated that you're competition for Fred Astaire when it comes to being suave, but I haven't called you any names, have I?"

"I wish I could have heard the ones inside your head the night of Gizmo's party, though."

Grace sighed tightly and frowned at the road ahead of them. "You never waste any time getting down to the nitty-gritty, do you? I should have realized that last night was merely the calm before the storm."

Luke shrugged. "I didn't feel like talking yesterday. Neither did you. Are we going to talk about it now?"

Grace hesitated. Talking about the awful party would surely bring on heated words. She didn't want that. Not this morning. Not with her head full of muddled emotions and the distinct longing to ask Luke to just hold her. She hadn't really been in his arms in so long! No, she didn't want to argue. She had to do a television interview shortly, and an argument would shake her confidence. With care, she said, "I don't think we ought to waste what little time we have by discussing that topic."

Luke didn't answer for a moment. He glanced sharply at Grace and nearly ran the car onto the shoulder. Jerking his attention back to the road, he easily straightened the Jaguar. His voice suddenly went dry. "We don't have to talk about anything if you'd rather not. But that's too bad. We've done okay up until now."

Grace swallowed with difficulty and agreed, "Conversation with you has been most enjoyable."

"Most enjoyable?" Luke repeated, testing her mood a little more. He sounded irritated suddenly. "Does that mean good?"

"I've liked being with you," Grace said stubbornly.

"Ooh!" he exclaimed, as if greatly enlightened. "You

mean the last couple of days haven't been too terrible for you, Dear Ms. Barrett?"

He wasn't calling her Princess anymore, Grace noted. Something had started to annoy him, that was certain. She found herself wishing that Luke would just leave well enough alone. Couldn't he see that her feelings for him had changed since they'd first met? In surprise, she asked, "Are you trying to pick a fight? All I said was that I liked your family. Why should that get you into such a hostile state?"

"I'm not being hostile," Luke said blithely. "You're the one with the white knuckles."

Grace relaxed her hands immediately, feeling foolishly guilty. She could come right out and tell him that she found him fascinating, but this didn't quite seem to be the time. Why did falling in love with a man have to be so damned unpleasant?

"Look," Luke said, undoubtedly misunderstanding all of her signs of dismay, "I took you to my home for lots of reasons, I suppose. One was that I needed some clean clothes, to tell you the truth, and I hadn't seen my folks in months. But I think your friend Lucy had the right idea."

"Lucy!" Grace said in surprise. "What has she got to do with you and me?"

"She had the right idea about you. You needed to see how the other half lives. What did you think, Ms. Barrett? Did the Lazurnovich family measure up? Or did we forget to put the soup spoon on the outside of the butter knife, and the napkin on—"

"I never once thought about table manners," Grace said quickly, telling the truth in the face of Luke's loss of good humor. "Not the whole time we were there."

"How come? That's supposed to be your job, isn't it?"

"Of course it isn't! I—I had other things to think about, and etiquette came pretty low on the program."

"What were you thinking about?" Luke asked, watching the road.

Grace sighed. "Your mother, mostly. I—she—oh, I don't know! Why didn't she *like* me?"

Luke began to laugh, but it sounded harsh. "What's the matter, Princess? Feeling uncomfortable? Unaccepted?"

"Yes, I guess that was it," Grace said, searching her mind for a way to express her feelings. "I didn't like the way I felt, the way she treated me. I was nervous and anxious, and I wanted her to like me, but she just didn't."

Luke did not argue the point. "Feeling left out?" he asked. "Shunned like a leper?"

"Well, that's a little strong, but yes, I—"

"How about that," Luke said lightly. He didn't look across at her, but observed, "For once, you were being judged by somebody else instead of the other way around."

Startled, Grace demanded, "What?"

"You heard me," Luke said. "Face it, Princess, you're a snob."

Grace's mouth popped open, but she composed herself and snapped it shut just as fast. "What's put you into such a mood, for heaven's sake?"

"Nothing," he snapped. "I knew all along it would come to this, I suppose, but I figured we could hold off the inevitable a little longer."

"Our differences?" Grace asked, going breathless. Did he have to bring all this up now? Today? Calling her a snob? What was he up to? Grace half turned in her seat to eye him speculatively. "It's been obvious from the very beginning that you and I are an unlikely pair, Laser. Did you imagine that one of us would manage to brainwash the other during a few days of delight in Cincinnati?"

"I never thought brainwashing was necessary for what we have—or had—between us. A few differences made things interesting. Now you've gotten stung, is that it? You didn't like it much when the tables got turned, and you found yourself being the object of criticism for once, did you? Have you got a different perspective on etiquette now, Ms. Barrett?"

Angry with his sarcasm, Grace snapped, "Because your mother didn't like me? I don't ruffle that easily, Luke. Look, my profession is trying to help people overcome touchy social situations in the most acceptable, painless ways possible. Etiquette isn't just good table manners; it's a set of rules for living in society that keeps everyone happy."

"Usually it's the people who make the rules who are happy. The rest of us feel stupid," he shot back. "It was nice to see you feeling stupid for once, Princess. I have to admit, I enjoyed seeing you squirm a little."

"Making anyone squirm is very bad manners," Grace retorted. "And lately, it's been me all the time, you know! Social rules were created to please everyone. To allow people to behave to please only themselves would produce anarchy. Which is precisely what was taking place at Gizmo Montgomery's party! You're damned right I was uncomfortable there! I was frightened!"

"You didn't look it. You looked like somebody had dragged in a dead skunk and laid it at your feet."

Grace ignored that taunt. "You can argue all you like. You won't convince me that I was wrong at that party, Luke. I hated it, and I won't go to another one. That wasn't just high spirits. To the uninitiated, it was pure self-indulgent savagery. Bad manners I can cope with, but the vulgar, ferocious, frightening behavior of those animals you call your friends was—"

"Okay, okay," Luke broke in. "I should have warned you. I should have protected you a little, I guess. But you had been rubbing my nose in the way I act and look and dress and—"

"I did not!" Grace cried. "I don't care how you look or dress, and after the first night in the restaurant, I made sure we took all our meals in private so you wouldn't feel uncomfortable."

"You watch me every second," Luke argued, "looking for things I do wrong."

"I do not!" Grace objected. She couldn't help watching him! She loved to watch him! He was beautiful and so darned attractive, and she was absorbed by his every move! But she couldn't tell him that. Not now. Now that he'd pushed and pushed until they were actually shouting at each other, Grace couldn't tell him that she was in love with him. He'd laugh. Certainly, he would! Without thinking, she muttered, "Oh, damn."

"This is it, isn't it?" Luke asked quietly.

Grace felt her stomach lurch. He was looking for a way to say good-bye, she realized. He'd had enough. He wanted to go home, get rid of her.

There was no future in their being together, Grace moaned to herself. They were too different. She had known it from the start, and so had Luke. They had had fun for a while. The sport of playing opposite sides had been a game, and making love had been spectacular. But their differences in lifestyle were just too extreme. Luke had known it long before she had. He wasn't going to waste any more of his time. This was the end of *The Luke and Gracie Show*.

She felt her throat tighten as she forced herself to reply, "If you think it's best."

"That we part company? Don't put it all on my shoulders, Princess."

Grace wanted to bite her lip, to clench her fists to keep her emotion inside. But he'd surely see the signs and make fun of her. He wanted to leave, but he wanted her to share the responsibility. She didn't have the strength to argue with him anymore. Quietly, she said, "All right, it *is* over, yes."

Luke let out a long, tense breath. Coldly, he said, "So you can go back to the likes of Kippy and his Harvard friends."

Grace turned at that and stared at Luke's averted profile. "Kip again? He's on your mind?"

"He must have been on yours lately," Luke snapped. "You've been comparing the two of us since last week, I'll bet."

"Kip was once the most important man in my life," Grace said sharply. "Of course I tend to think of him when I'm around other men."

"Pretty sad comparison, I suppose."

"Yes," Grace said acidly, plunging into the discussion with all her manufactured hostility now. If Luke wanted to part, she would make it easier! Matching his sarcasm, she said, "The comparison was most unpleasant, as a matter of fact!"

"Kip must be a real cutie," Luke decided. "Very proper and polite. 'Shall we retire for the evening, Grace darling? Will you help me with my cummerbund, sweetheart? Shall we have the maid turn down the sheets? Please lie still, and maybe you won't enjoy this too much.'"

Before he got too crude, Grace said distinctly, "Luke, shut up."

"Shut *up?*" Luke repeated on an astonished laugh. "Dear Ms. Barrett tells me to shut up?"

"My relationship with Kip is over, and it's not any of your business anyway. Please stop it."

"You're right, it's none of my business. What *does* concern me is what happened between you and me in these last few days."

"I'd rather not talk about it," Grace said swiftly.

"I'm sure," Luke agreed heavily. "Sleeping with a football player will undoubtedly go down in your diary as a real walk on the wild side. Did you like it, Ms. Barrett? Did I perform well enough to—"

"Luke—"

"You were well satisfied," he said harshly. "Unless you're very good at faking sexual excitement."

"Stop it!" Grace shouted in anger. Her voice went too high and cracked. "I mean it, Luke! Don't say another word!"

Amazingly, he obeyed and remained silent.

"I hate this part of you," Grace said breathlessly "You're an absolute bastard when you want to be—and you take such pleasure in shocking me!"

"And what happened in our bed in Cincinnati—"

"Does not make up for the way you're treating me now!"

"But you did like it?" Luke demanded. "Was it the best sex you ever had, Dear Ms. Barrett? Are you going back to New York to tell all your—"

"I told you at the time I was going to regret making love with you," Grace interrupted curtly. Inside, she felt the tears starting to build and build. Why did he have to be so horrible? To the window, she said, "I didn't really believe myself at the time, but it's certianly true now. I wish I'd never met you!"

"It was a cultural exchange, remember?"

"Shut up!" Grace cried desperately.

"Shut up *again?* You're really slipping, Dear Ms. Barrett. Look, in another ten miles, we'll be at the station and you can go. I'd let you out here so you could walk, but it's not a nice neighborhood and I've got a few tiny grains of the gentleman in me. Think you can hold out for ten minutes? Or has your tolerance for the common people just run out?"

"You're not common," Grace said, more to herself than to him. "If I've made you feel common, that was my fault and I'm sorry. For a while, I thought you were a good man, Luke Lazurnovich. But you were mean and unfeeling to me at Gizmo's party, and I should have packed my bags that night and left you."

"An error in your otherwise flawless judgment," Luke agreed. "We could have spared each other all these long hours of suffering if you'd done that."

He must really hate her, Grace decided. She must have really hurt his feelings and made him feel small. To wound a man's ego was the worse possible thing a woman could do. Grace felt she ought to know. She had killed Kip's self-confidence rather effectively, and now she was working on Luke's. Fortunately, he was strong enough to order her out of his life before he got too bad. Grace respected him for that.

So she held her tongue. Perhaps Luke ought to have the last word one more time.

He drove in silence for a couple more miles, watching the side streets. When he pulled the car along the curb finally, Grace had her door open before he set the brake. She got out onto the sidewalk and went to the back of the car for her luggage. Luke drew up his long legs and got out also, shivering once in the cold air. As usual, he did not put on his jacket. Shoulders hunched against the chill, he walked to the back of the car, flipping through his keys for the one to the trunk. Without a word to Grace, he opened the trunk.

Grace grabbed the handles of both her cases before he could. She hefted them awkwardly out of the car and retreated to the sidewalk, then turned.

Luke waited, his hand on the upraised trunk lid for a moment. His eyes were half closed but very alert, watching her face.

"You've parked in another no-parking zone," Grace noted composedly, gesturing at the sign nearby.

"One more ticket won't matter."

"Do you suppose," she asked, her voice hard with the effort it was taking to control herself, "that one more kiss would matter either?"

Luke blinked, his face slackening just a fraction in surprise.

"Never mind," she said quickly. "I can see you'd rather not. I just thought that—"

He slammed the trunk lid and came to the curb. He interrupted Grace by taking her elbows, one in each of his hands. He pulled her to the edge of the curb, and the six inches' difference between the street where he stood and the sidewalk where Grace remained brought them almost eye to eye. Luke's gaze didn't waver but sought hers as if magnetized. His grip was hard, almost painful, but she didn't flinch. She struggled with the icy stiffness in her throat and the boiling hot tears that threatened to break through at any moment.

Softly, so softly that above the street noise the word was hardly audible, Luke said her name. He murmured simply "Grace," and then he kissed her on the mouth.

His lips were warm and familiar, wonderfully firm and gently coaxing. Grace closed her eyes and weakened, letting the sweetness of his kiss wash through her. His body, strong and lithe, beckoned to hers, and she stepped cautiously nearer until he warmed her limbs with his. She longed to drop her suitcases and throw her arms around his neck, but she curbed the treacherous impulse. He wanted this to be good-bye. She wouldn't fight him anymore.

Luke pressed deeply into her mouth, urging her lips to part and accept his final tender exploration. The moment lengthened and reality slipped away. Grace knew dimly that she was trembling with her inevitable involuntary response to his sensuality. Smoothly, Luke lessened the kiss until all that remained was the earth-shattering gentleness that turned Grace's heart over with a painful thump. When he drew back, her inhaled breath sounded like a sob. Luke planted a last, almost reverent kiss on her forehead, then slackened his hold on her.

Grace blinked her eyes open. Too late, she realized they were full of tears.

Luke reacted at once, catching her hand in surprise. "Princess!"

Grace hurried to back away from him, tugging out of his grasp. "It's nothing. How awful! Crying in the street is worse than kissing—ask my mother any day! Good-bye, Luke."

"Princess . . ." He started up onto the curb.

"Good-bye, good-bye," Grace said desperately, backing away before he grabbed her. Did he want to humiliate her for good? Drag all sorts of embarrassing confessions out of her before he left? Hastily, she said, "Don't chase me, please. This is bad enough. Go back to Pittsburgh. Write me a Dear Ms. Barrett letter sometime!"

"Princess!" Luke shouted after her.

But Grace didn't look back. Leaving Luke to argue with the policeman who had pulled his cruiser in behind the illegally parked Jaguar, she ran up the stairs to the television studio, blinking back the fresh onslaught of tears that threatened to spill from her burning eyes.

CHAPTER TWELVE

"Texas," drawled Lucy Simons as she lay back on the luxurious hotel bed on the following Friday afternoon, "is marvelous. Did I tell you about the cowboys in the bar last night?"

"No," Grace said, hanging her suit jacket in the closet. She crossed back to the dresser and picked up her half-drained coffee cup from the room-service tray. "But knowing you, I think I can guess what happened."

"They're *marvelously* disgusting," Lucy said, her dark eyes sparkling with devious delight. Lucy was a great believer in the New York Cheesecake Diet, and her not-quite-slender figure reflected her occasional moments of overindulgence. Lucy's heart-shaped face and dark eyes, her cunning doll's face on a soft and femininely unsuntanned body, was some men's idea of sexiness. Lucy frequently cashed in on her innocent good looks before her quick tongue changed the picture. She studied her fingernails. "I was actually tempted to throw tequila in the face of one of them."

"It's not like you to be prudent," Grace said dryly. "What stopped you?"

Lucy propped her arms behind her head, displacing her luscious tumble of blue-black hair. "He got me first, as a matter of fact. Served me right, because by then I had stooped even lower than he had. Delightful man. He bought me a new dress this morning to make up for it."

"Lucy, that's more than disgusting," Grace said after swallowing a slug of coffee. She set down the cup and returned to her half-empty suitcase. "It's downright sickening, in fact. Don't tell me another word."

"As you wish," Lucy agreed, and she yawned prettily. Coming up on her elbow, she watched Grace place her makeup bag on the dressing table. Sounding deceptively uninterested, Lucy suggested, "Perhaps you'll do some talking now."

"About what?"

"Dear Gray," Lucy complained emphatically, "you've been tearing around the country for two entire weeks with barely three phone calls to my office the whole time. Besides tonight's party, half my reason for leaving Manhattan was to find out what you've been up to. I'm positively bursting with curiosity! As they say out here, what gives, partner?"

Grace opened the top drawer and threw two pairs of panties in it. "Nothing!"

"Don't give me that," Lucy said languidly. "I know more than you think, so fess up. You never did explain what happened to Lombardi the football player."

"We parted company," Grace said shortly, snatching up her nightgown from the suitcase.

"Oh?"

"In St. Louis," Grace added, hurling it angrily into the drawer. "I haven't heard from him since."

"I see," Lucy said in a new tone of voice.

Grace swung around and glared at her friend. "What does *that* mean?"

"You tell me," Lucy said indulgently, not moving from her ultrarelaxed position on Grace's bed. Lucy had a Cheshire-cat smile that was perfection, and she used it now.

"Don't try to convince me that this mood of yours was caused by your very first airplane ride since junior high, my friend. And you're not drunk enough to use that as an excuse."

Grace thrust her shaking hand into her atypically un-combed hair and brushed it back from her face. "I did hate that flight from Chicago! I'll take an ox cart back to New York before I'll get on another one of those death traps!"

Lucy shrugged. "It couldn't be helped. The party was scheduled for tonight, so I booked you on the airline. I must admit, I never expected to see you so bleary-eyed when I met you at the airport, but—"

"I was bleary-eyed from booze," Grace said firmly. "Don't imagine I'm having some kind of ridiculous emotional crisis or anything!"

"Why should I imagine that? Just because you broke into tears on the telephone two nights ago, before I even mentioned the flight to Dallas? Which is something you haven't done since Harold Pickney-Bowen didn't ask you to the spring frolic."

Grace sat down on the edge of the bed. Being with Lucy had triggered all those emotions Grace had successfully buried since her Tuesday crying jag. The nausea from flying and too much liquor too early in the day wasn't helping her stability, either. She blew a sigh, as if all her tensions could be expended by releasing that pent-up breath. It didn't work. The lump was still inside, a leaden ball of unpleasantness that had lodged halfway between her throat and her stomach. It hadn't budged since she'd left Luke on the street in St. Louis.

"Well," Lucy asked, "what happened?"

Staring straight ahead, Grace said evenly, "I fell in love with him, Luce."

Lucy sat up quickly and abandoned her cool voice of reason. "I didn't realize! How nice, Gray!"

Grace smiled ruefully and shook her head. "It's supposed to be, isn't it? You always read about painful love affairs, but I never imagined it had to *hurt* like this!"

Lucy crawled to the edge of the bed and put her plump

arm around Grace's shoulders. "Darling! What's wrong?"

Grace leaned thankfully into her friend. "Nothing. Everything. I fell in love with a man who's so wrong for me that it wasn't funny after a while. We both knew it was a—a—"

"Hopeless passion?"

Grace laughed weakly. "You're still a fink. Yes, it was hopeless. He decided to break things off, so I graciously went along with his wishes and continued with my tour—"

"Wait a minute," Lucy said. *"He* broke things off?"

"Yep. Funny, isn't it? You'd think *he*'d be the one who wouldn't quite measure up to *my* standards, but actually, it was quite the opposite. He called me a snob and said goodbye."

"Hmm," Lucy said thoughtfully.

"And I've been miserable ever since," Grace said flatly. "Oh, Luce, why did you make me come on this stupid tour in the first place? Is it really going to sell tons of books?"

"Yes," Lucy said positively, sitting up again. She gave Grace a pat on her back. "You hit the best-seller lists this week, as predicted. And I think you're soon going to admit that this tour has changed your life."

"Not for the better," Grace shot back as Lucy rolled off the bed and got up. "Unless a permanent state of spinsterhood is good news."

"I wouldn't make any bets if I were you," Lucy advised. She checked her reflection in the mirror and straightened her hair before turning back to Grace. "Now, listen up, Gray. Change into your best duds and we'll go directly downstairs. Are you sober enough yet? You won't throw up into a potted palm, will you? The party has already started, and I promised a lot of people that you'd show your lovelorn face."

"Who? What people?"

"Your mother, for one."

Grace groaned and slumped forward, her face in her hands.

"Easy there," Lucy advised. "Gray, your formidable

mother has been marvelous since we got here. She's risen to a new height in my esteem since Wednesday. You're going to be proud to be her daughter before this is over."

Grace lifted her face and eyed Lucy without cheer. "All right, all right. Who else? What publicity stunt did you finally devise for tonight's party? Are the networks beating down the hotel doors to cover our celebration?"

"As a matter of fact, the lobby is mobbed with press," Lucy said smugly. "Which is why I smuggled you in the back way. This party is going to be a triumph, my friend! That syndicated evening entertainment program is here, cameras ready!"

"How did you manage it?" Grace inquired, staying on the bed while Lucy headed for the door. "What brought the press to a book party, anyway?"

Lucy waved airily. "You wait and see. It was a brilliant idea for an etiquette party. Put on your prettiest dress and be prepared to be swept off your feet, little filly! Texas awaits! I'll go change and see you in a few minutes!"

Lucy paused at the door and whisked a single bloom from the vase of flowers that stood on the pedestal there. Comically, she clenched it in her teeth and swept out of the room, closing the door and leaving Grace alone.

Aimlessly, Grace got up and wandered to the door. She leaned there and sighed dispiritedly. It was no use. She didn't feel the least bit like celebrating. And Mother would undoubtedly be a pain in the neck. Grace pulled a flower from the vase, just as Lucy had done. Tulips, they were, vivid red ones. Grace held one to her nose thoughtfully.

She should have thanked Lucy for the flowers, she thought suddenly. The card lay on the pedestal beside the vase. Grace picked it up again and read it: "Welcome to Dallas. L."

Dear Lucy. A girl couldn't have a nicer friend at a time like this. Lucy didn't mind her faults and would hold her hand while Grace recovered from being jilted by Luke "the Laser" Lazurnovich.

She had better reciprocate and do Lucy a good turn, she supposed. The party awaited her, and Lucy had gone to a lot of trouble to organize it. Grace began to unbutton her blouse, heading for her closet again. The red wool dress would do. A thought struck her. Grace stopped. She turned back on the vase of flowers and stared at the card again. "Welcome to Dallas. L."

Couldn't be.

Could it?

Grace tore out of her blouse and ran to the closet. It could be. It certainly could. The heck with her red wool dress! She yanked her blue silk sheath off its hanger. It was a slim, draping dress with a dusty pink obi that clasped her waist and drew the eye down her figure. Yes, this dress was perfect. In seconds, Grace had it over her head and was tugging the delicate fabric down over her curves. Perfect. She flew to the mirror and sat down, dumping the contents of her makeup bag all over the dressing table. Hurrying, she made up her face, then hung her head upside down and brushed her hair vigorously. Shaking it, she recombed the top and let it go. A little wild, a little sexy. Perfect.

Rose shoes, a small clutch handbag. Grace met Lucy in the hallway and dragged her by the arm into the elevator. "Lucy Simons, tell me immediately what's going on."

"Going on?" Lucy asked, staggering against the back railing of the elevator as Grace whirled around and jabbed the button. "What's gotten into you, Gray?"

Grace spun on Lucy and advanced with a menacing finger pointed straight at Lucy's nose. "What have you been hiding? You said you knew more than I thought you knew, so I'm demanding to know what you know!"

"My dear," Lucy said, smiling, "I believe you need some more coffee. You're raving!"

"What's your publicity stunt, Lucille? Have you planned to humiliate me in public?"

"On the contrary, I'm going to elevate you to the status of miracle worker. Only you're going to have to share the honors with your mother tonight."

"Mother! What's she got to do with anything?"

The elevator arrived at the mezzanine, and the doors

began to open. Lucy ducked out of Grace's range and cried, "There she is! At the head of the receiving line. Ask her yourself, Gray. Oh, smile for the cameras first, please!"

Flashbulbs blinded Grace the instant she stepped off the elevator. An orchestra struck up a lively tune. Polite applause and a few raucous cheers from the back of the cavernlike room confirmed Grace's belief that the party was very large. Perhaps two hundred people had crowded into the elegantly decorated ballroom to celebrate the arrival of *Ms. Barrett's Etiquette for Every Occasion* on the best-seller lists.

Flashbulb blindness caught Grace offguard, but with Lucy's hand drawing her, she plunged into the crowd. Her mother's voice warbled high but commandingly: "Grace, darling, this way! Here, lovey!"

It was indeed Mother, looking like the Queen of the World, or at least the Queen Mother, in one of her taffeta-and-pillbox-hat ensembles, complete with feathers and the sparkling diamonds of Great-grandmother Lendwell's brooch. Grace noted that her mother's complexion was powdery-pale, although her blue eyes were lavishly lined and mascaraed. Her mouth wasn't pinched for once, though, and the tip of her nose was adorably pink, a sure sign that Mother had been sipping champagne. She looked happy, in fact— a rare phenomenon.

Mother caught Grace's hands and they traded pecks on the cheek. She was several inches shorter than Grace, so her kiss barely made contact with Grace's makeup. As usual, she spoke only in exclamations. "Lovey, you can't imagine such excitement! Lucille's outdone herself! Are you ready? Such publicity! This way! See what Lucy's brought! I've trained them myself! Such fun! Like the old days of Mrs. Barrett's Etiquette School! Look!"

It was Luke, of course.

Grace gasped a breath to steady her suddenly light head. Luke's smile was shy and a little guilty but quivering at the edges, as though he were about to burst into laughter. His eyes, meeting Grace's over her mother's energetic head, sparkled defiantly.

Belatedly, Grace realized that he was dressed in the spiffiest black dinner jacket and starchiest white shirt this side of Fred Astaire. He looked devilishly handsome, unbelievably dashing. He'd even shaved.

"Go on," Mother prodded him in a hissing whisper, jabbing him in the ribs from below with her elbow.

Thus reminded of his manners, Luke took a pace forward and grasped Grace's hand in his. His lines contained the barest stiffness of well-rehearsed words, but his smile was definitely genuine. "Good evening, Ms. Barrett. Perhaps you remember that we've met before? My name is Lucius Lazurnovich."

"Lucius *Baines* Lazurnovich," Grace corrected shakily. Trying to manage a smile that didn't tremble, she said, "Yes, of course I—I remember, Mr. Lazurnovich."

Responding to another jab from Mother's discreet elbow, Luke tugged Grace into the crowd. "Perhaps you'd permit me to introduce some of my friends, Ms. Barrett. They've all come to wish you well—at Miss Simons's invitation, of course. May I present Terrence Mitchell?"

Blood Mitchell, looking serious and totally at ease in his dinner jacket and bow tie, reached for Grace's hand and bowed over it. He played his part to the hilt, saying in formal tones, "How do you do, Ms. Barrett? Were your travel arrangements satisfactory, I hope?"

"Yes, thank you," Grace responded to this transformed football player with a dazed smile.

"And Mr. James McCoy," Luke said, guiding Grace down the line of tuxedoed men.

He's Dead Jim McCoy blanched openly, for his lines hadn't been as carefully planned as the others, it seemed. He glanced nervously down at Mother Barrett, who shot him with a deadly look. Snapping to attention, he said in a rush, "Good evening, Ms. Barrett. Nice weather in Texas, huh?"

"Very nice, Mr. McCoy," Grace agreed politely. "So good to see you again."

He's Dead must have panicked, because his eyes widened

at her response. He hadn't been prepared to think on his feet. Stumbling, he said, "Uh, yeah. Same here."

Next came Gizmo Montgomery, and then Leon Murzowski, both with dinner jackets and sweating palms. They recited their lines and nervously glanced at Mother Barrett when they were finished, apparently to be sure they hadn't goofed. Grace noticed that as Luke led her down the lineup, her mother gave each man a surreptitious pat to praise him for his good behavior. The football players visibly relaxed when they realized they had passed muster before Grace, the formidable Mrs. Barrett, and the blazing lights of the watching television cameras.

Finally, there were no more people to greet, and the crowd seemed to close in around them. Someone pressed a dainty glass cup of champagne punch into Grace's hand. The bright television lights shut down, and the party began in earnest. A waiter floated by with a silver tray of watercress sandwiches. Grace saw Blood Mitchell reach for the tray, his huge hand capable of grabbing half a dozen sandwiches easily. Mother spotted him with her eagle eye, however, and Blood froze, remembering that he'd better watch himself. He took one sandwich and a pretty little napkin. The sandwich disappeared in one mighty swallow, and then Blood looked at the napkin with puzzlement, as if wondering what to do with it now. Luke headed past him, slipped the napkin out from between Blood's fingers, and concealed it in his pocket, slicker than a pickpocket.

Then Luke turned and took Grace's elbow. She turned to him and glanced up at his face uncertainly. By instinct, he took her other hand, so that they stood together in the milling crush, looking deeply into each other's eyes.

"Oh, Luke," Grace said first, sounding foolish.

"Surprised?" he asked.

"Knocked right off my pedestal," she replied, feeling stronger. He didn't hate her. By some miracle, he was smiling.

"Good," he said, removing the champagne cup from her hand and setting it on the nearest table. "I've been there myself lately. Princess, I know this is your party, and I promised Lucy I'd let you do what you have to do, but—"

"Lucy?" Grace interrupted, over the noise of the crowd. "Are the two of you in cahoots? You didn't show up here on your own?"

Luke grinned. "Are you kidding? As soon as you walked into that TV station in St. Louis, I got in my car and called her on the phone for help."

"After settling up on yet another parking ticket, I'll bet!"

Luke's hand strayed quickly to her face, molding to her cheek as he spoke. The gesture was gentle, and it brought a surge of hope inside of Grace. His voice so low that only the two of them could hear, he murmured, "You've cost me a small fortune in parking tickets, my love, and I couldn't care less. Princess, how soon can I club you over the head and drag you out by your hair without offending these high-society dames?"

Grace smiled and leaned into him. "Oh, Luke."

He nodded quickly. "We've got to talk."

Lucy must have overheard: Arriving at Luke's elbow just then, she shouted above the party noise, "You can talk later. There are two hundred guests here to meet the author. Grace, go do your duty and let me entertain this man for a while."

"Lucy—" Grace protested.

"Lucy—" Luke began, in just the same pleading tone.

Lucy laughed and tugged at Luke's arm. "Come on, Lombardi. I've got a hundred things to tell you, and the music's perfect for dancing."

"Hold it," Grace objected. There were limits to even the best friendships, and Lucy's track record with the opposite sex spoke for itself. "Just a minute, Lucille!"

Lucy sent a flirtatious flutter of eyelashes up at Luke. "You're not scared, are you, Lombardi? Would you like to hear about Boom-Boom Barrett's riotous days at school?"

"Boom-Boom?" Luke repeated, with an astonished look down at Grace. "Really? Is there a side of you I don't know yet, Princess?"

"Lucy!" Grace said fiercely. Maybe Luke wouldn't think

her schoolgirl escapades all that riotous, but she'd be embarrassed for him to learn about them anyway.

"Come along, Miss Simons," Luke said, dropping Grace
and taking Lucy's elbow with alacrity. "Let's dance."

CHAPTER THIRTEEN

THE PARTY WAS going strong, Grace realized. Tuxedo-clad waiters were circulating with silver trays, distributing tiny glasses of champagne punch to the guests. As Grace watched, Blood Mitchell took a glass and—realizing how tiny it was in his huge hand—stared down at it as if he'd suddenly found himself holding the delicate egg of a nearly extinct tropical bird. He looked faintly stunned, then drank off the punch in one effortless swallow. The small alcohol content of the beverage must have helped to steady his nerves, for he summoned a noble expression and gazed out on the party from his great height. He looked, for a moment, like a serene African prince.

He's Dead Jim McCoy wasn't having such good luck. He found himself pinned between the watercress sandwiches and Mother Barrett, who was keeping a discerning eye on his every move. He's Dead was clearly uncomfortable, his already ruddy face ashine with nervous perspiration. He tugged at the stiff collar of his shirt. Mother discreetly elbowed him to put a stop to such behavior.

"Look relaxed, now, James," she admonished in a barely audible undertone. Her upward gaze at He's Dead, however, packed the voltage of the Sing Sing electric chair. "A gentleman should always strive to look sedate, remember."

He's Dead, looking as if he'd actually much rather be in Sing Sing than this particular party, said solicitously, "Yes, Mrs. Barrett, ma'am."

"You needn't call me both Mrs. Barrett and ma'am," Mother murmured promptly, laying her hand on He's Dead's arm. "We've discussed that before, James."

Her slight hand must have caused still another jolt of electricity for He's Dead, because he immediately snapped to attention. "Y-yes, ma'am."

"Perhaps you should consider a longer course, James," Mother said decisively. "You could come back to Connecticut with me, if you like. I have much better facilities there for teaching good manners, you understand. It's so difficult when my only help comes from poorly trained hotel employees. My own servants are so much more efficient when it comes to educating young people like yourself in the arts of gracious living. You must come, James."

He's Dead, in the act of stealthily swiping a glass of punch from a passing waiter, promptly bobbled the dainty glass at Mother's subtle command. He made a swift grab to catch it, but the cup upended, sending a spray of punch down the front of his ruffled shirt. He's Dead lost his cool "Aw, for—"

Blood, sensing an outburst of less-than-gracious language, grabbed He's Dead by his elbow and gave it a mighty squeeze, putting a stop to the obscenities before they got started. Blood pasted a smile on his face and turned to Mother. "Oh, such an unfortunate accident, Mrs. Barrett. Perhaps James and I should step outside for a moment and take care of this little problem."

"By all means," Mother said, although it was obvious from her expression that she intended to keep all the football players under her close observation for the duration of the party.

He's Dead heaved a sigh of relief and practically dragged

Blood toward the nearest door. It was clear to Grace that Mother had been a merciless drill instructor, the likes of which even professional athletes had never seen. The tortures of football training camp could hardly compare to the rigors of one of Mrs. Barrett's excruciating etiquette courses.

The party itself had all the signs of a Mrs. Barrett bash. The guests were elegantly dressed, their manners impeccable. The foods were delicately attractive as well as delicious, the wine punch perfectly chilled and with just the right bite of good French champagne. Candelabra, the sparkle of good crystal, immaculate white linens, and soft but jaunty music provided by a discreetly small orchestra all provided the appropriate atmosphere. Even the mingling football players looked like a part of it all, elegantly garbed in their black evening clothes, which had undoubtedly been chosen by Mother herself. It all looked very familiar to Grace, who'd been attending her mother's oh-so-proper parties since she was old enough to hold a teacup. Now, however, Grace longed to be as far from a huge crowd as she could get. She looked yearningly after Luke and Lucy, happily in each other's arms, chattering like old friends already and apparently oblivious to the party around them.

"Grace, lovey!" Mother cried, lurching to Grace's side with a fluted champagne glass clutched in her pudgy jewel-encrusted fingers. Now that her charges were sufficiently launched into polite society, Mother was feeling flush, it appeared. "Darling, we've had *such* a good time these last few days!" she gushed.

Sending one last longing gaze after Luke and Lucy, Grace said distractedly, "Hello, Mother."

"That darling Luke tells me that you know each other!" Mother exclaimed. "How did you ever *meet* such a man?"

"What?" Grace asked, finally hearing her mother's voice through the hubbub of the party. "What did you say about Luke?

Mother took Grace's arm and guided her to a table laden with scrumptious-looking canapés. "My dear, he's so sweet! Such a darling boy! He works so hard and—well, I swear he never *heard* of the word *surrender!*"

"Exactly what has gone on here the last few days?" Grace asked, ignoring the food and turning on her mother with a determination to understand the whole story.

"It was Lucille's idea," Mother said with enthusiasm, selecting a mushroom cap stuffed with crab filling. "And I think Luke's, too. We needed a publicity stunt, so they corralled some of Luke's friends and we conducted an old-fashioned etiquette course. Isn't that a wonderful word? *Corralled?* That's Texan, you know." She popped the mushroom into her mouth and sighed with pleasure as it melted on her tongue.

Grace handed her a napkin. "Do you mean that you taught all those football players how to behave at a party like this?"

Mother nodded vigorously, dabbing her mouth with dainty movements. "And we saw that they were properly dressed and combed, and we rehearsed their lines to perfection. I must say, that Mr. Mitchell was a bit of a problem at first, and Mr. McCoy needed some extra tutoring, but with Luke's help—he kept them all in line for me until they bought me my whistle—I managed quite well, don't you think?" Mother snatched the gold-plated whistle that hung on a chain around her neck. It had looked like a piece of jewelry to Grace up until now, but she realized as Mother waggled it in the air that it was indeed a football coach's whistle. "It was quite fun and most worthwhile. These young men learned a great deal."

"More than you know, Mother," Grace said wryly. "This is an 'after' picture. You should have seen their party manners before!"

Mother dropped the whistle and gave an airy wave of her hand. "They've all turned over new leaves, darling!"

"Why?" Grace demanded in bewilderment. "Why should they go through all this? Has somebody paid them? Or maybe blackmailed them into coming?"

"Of course not, darling!" Mother gave a tinkling laugh. She selected a celery stick with something orange lavishly slathered on it. "They're helping us as a favor to Luke! And he was so determined that this party go off without a hitch—that's also Texas talk. Oh, did I tell you about the gentleman from Houston whom I met last night? He's—"

"Mother!" Grace cried in frustration. "Why is Luke so determined to have a good party? What's going on?"

Mother took a crunch of her celery and blinked at Grace in surprise. "Why, darling, I think he's in love with you, of course!"

"Of course," Grace said dazedly.

Mother patted Grace's arm. "And he's *such* a darling! So hardworking! So determined! So much fun! And he always has these sinfully rich butter cookies in his pockets that I just *swoon* over—"

"I don't believe it," Grace said, shaking her head, eyes closed. "I really don't. He's won you over."

"My darling! Did you think I was such a prude? Why shouldn't you have a man who looks as tremendously gorgeous as he does? My dear! Have you *seen* him in the shorts he runs in? My smelling salts, *please!* Lucy tells me he's called a hunk. Disgusting word, but so apropos! Darling Grace, how wonderful for you!"

Grace began to laugh weakly. "Mother, I never imagined that you looked at men as anything but a source of polite dinner conversation."

"Darling," Mother said wisely, with a reprimanding shake of her pretty head, "did you suppose I found you under a cabbage leaf?"

"But—"

Mother interrupted swiftly, "Darling, your father and I outgrew each other, that is all. He's found his niche in life— heaven help his digestion—and I'm finding mine. That gentleman from Houston I was telling you about just might be my second opportunity in life. If so, I'm going to grab it. You should do the same. Forget that Peers fellow you were seeing. He was a stuffy old coot before he was thirty! You've got your chance for something better."

With a smile, Grace shook her head. "Mother, I feel as though I'm just starting to know you. Can I buy you a drink?"

Mother laughed. "I've had quite enough, darling. And you've got better things to do than stand in the corner and talk with your mother. Go find Luke and see if he's still interested."

"But this party! I should really go around and—"

"Shake hands? Make small talk? Darling, who cares how many books you sell? Go get Luke away from Lucille before she does something unforgivably common—like undressing him in a public place. Go on. I'll hold the press at bay. I can manage it, you know!"

Yes, Grace decided, if her mother could train the likes of Blood Mitchell and He's Dead Jim McCoy to behave like human beings, she could certainly persuade the press to find their stories somewhere else. Grace bent and gave her mother a quick but genuine kiss on her cheek. "Thanks, Mother."

"Run along," Mother said fondly.

Grace found Luke and Lucy on the dance floor. They were giggling together, and when the music provided the right opportunity, Luke bent Lucy over backward in a classic dip. She laughed in delight, and then he spun her away again. Grace caught up with them halfway across the parquet floor.

"Gray!" Lucy cried, catching sight of her. "Aren't you supposed to be hostessing? Acting like the celebrated author, you foolish thing? Go away and let me entertain Luke awhile. You've been neglecting him shamefully."

"Nuts to that," Grace said flatly, and she hooked her thumb to tell Lucy to get lost. "It's your party, you man-hunting witch. Go be your own hostess."

"Ladies, please," Luke admonished lightly. "Is this the proper way to talk? Can't we settle this politely?"

"How do you feel about ménages à trois?" Lucy inquired with pretended sultriness as she blinked up at him. "Or are you old-fashioned like Grace?"

"Definitely old-fashioned," Luke said promptly, letting Lucy go. He reached for Grace's hand and drew her to him.

Lucy sighed with disappointment. "Are there no adventurers left in the world? Am I alone in my search for excitement and variety?"

"Go find McCoy," Luke advised, gathering Grace up to dance with her. "I think you'll meet your match."

Lucy wriggled her eyebrows lasciviously. "Say no more! Good-bye, you two. Don't get married without me, all right?"

Luke swept Grace into the crowd, holding her body snugly to his. His arm was warm and familiar behind her back, and his hand had slipped naturally into a tantalizing spot just behind her breast. He held her so firmly that she laid her head on his shoulder and sighed in a kind of relief. Just touching him again was heaven. She relaxed in his arms and moved gently with his easy rhythm.

He danced—not expertly, but serviceably—around the perimeter of the floor, heading for the elevators.

"Princess," he said, his voice barely a whisper in her ear.

"Yes," Grace responded, shifting her arms even higher and more securely around his neck. "Let's go upstairs and talk."

"Your party . . . ?"

"We can come back later."

Luke laughed a little and shook his head. "If we go upstairs, I don't have any intention of coming back."

With a smile, Grace tipped her head and met Luke's warm, heavy-lidded eyes. "Really?"

He tightened his arm even more, until their thighs burned together and their bodies met pliantly. "Really. In fact, if we go up there, I'm not sure I'm going to have the self-restraint to say all the things I want to say."

"Self-restraint?"

"Exactly. I won't want to talk."

They danced their way into an open elevator. Smiling, Grace pressed a button over his shoulder and agreed, "I've got an open mind, you know."

Luke laughed.

As the door hummed quietly closed behind them, shutting off the party noise in one silencing rush, Luke gathered her up and kissed her. Excitement and delight churned in Grace's veins. Her emotions welled up so forcefully that she thought her throat would burst. He wanted her. He wasn't angry any longer. He didn't hate her for her pretentious ways and icy manners. He'd seen a deeper part of her, she was sure.

His kiss was warm with tenderness, not passion alone. His mouth melted deliciously on hers, his tongue playing elusively to find hers.

Luke cupped her head, slipping his fingers through her silky hair until he could hold her inescapably in his kiss. His breath had stopped, but beneath her hand Grace could feel the tearing beat of his heart.

At last he released her lips and gazed into her eyes. "I hated being without you."

Grace caught an uneven breath, unable to tear her eyes from Luke's smoldering gaze. "I've been miserable, too. Luke—"

"I know, I know. We said some things we shouldn't have."

"I'm sorry. I—"

"So am I," he said quickly, not allowing her to get her explanation out. "I behaved like an idiot in Detroit, and I know I was wrong."

"No," Grace said firmly, hugging him. "I was wrong, too. I shouldn't have put you in a position of choosing between me and your friends. It was your party. I shouldn't have made any judgments."

"Princess, I can't change overnight," Luke said, pressing her head close to his. "I am what I am, and a hundred more weeks like this one with your mother isn't going to make me into somebody like Kip."

"I don't want Kip," Grace whispered, running her fingers through his curling hair. "Luke, I want you. I love you. Honestly, I do."

He laughed, sounding exuberant, then held her away again until he could see her eyes. His own were sparkling with life. "With a few reservations?"

"With no reservations," Grace retorted.

Luke blew a long sigh, his smile growing. He shook his head. "I love you, too, Princess. I don't know how it happened."

"Are we *that* different?"

"We're different all right," he agreed slowly. "Can you stand it?"

"I think," Grace said in a low, peaceful voice that reflected her innermost thoughts, "that I can learn to thrive on it."

Heaven only knew how long they stood together. Finally, Luke realized that the elevator door had long been standing open, and he pulled Grace out into the hall. Regaining her wits, she led him to the door of her room. She didn't bother with the light switch. The curtains were parted slightly so that the bright lights from the street far below created just enough illumination for her to see Luke's expressive features. In seconds, they were in each other's arms again.

"Do you mean it?" Luke asked softly, appreciatively tracing the planes of her face with the tip of his nose. "Do you think we'll be okay together?"

"Better than okay." Grace smiled, eyes closed as she endured the sweet sensations his gentle caresses evoked. Her own hands strayed automatically down his chest. "I've missed you too much to want to live without you, Luke. I want you so much."

He gave a pretended groan in the semidarkness. "There's just one problem that's keeping me from putting you on that bed over there."

"I'm a great problem-solver."

Smiling and trying to look miserable at the same time, he said plaintively, "I can't get out of this crazy cummerbund!"

Laughing, Grace began to oblige, and Luke twisted so that she could release him from the dapper garment. When it had drifted to the floor, she slipped his dinner jacket off his shoulders. He was already unfastening the button at the nape of her slender neck. Enjoying the sight of Luke's body coming out of its wrapping, like a much longed-for gift, Grace unbuttoned each of his shirt studs and pressed soft, joyful kisses on his skin. She loved him. She was delirious in his presence. Whatever their differences in personality, she was sure they could overcome them. This feeling—this strong, undeniable yearning for him—was too much to toss aside. He was perfect. Strong and good and kind.

With a reverence that was tempered only by the swiftness

of their actions, they undressed each other and moved to the bed, hand in hand. There, Grace turned into his arms again, relishing the hard contours of his body as they matched her softer, suppler curves. Luke's hands passed down her shoulders, caressing her arms, until he touched her breasts and remained there to enjoy their taut peaks. A flood of sensual pleasure caught Grace like a cresting wave, and she closed her eyes involuntarily.

Bending his head, Luke brushed her curving lips with his. "Don't," he said. "I love to watch your eyes, Princess. Share it with me."

Grace opened her eyes and smiled anew. "You say the nicest things. It surprises me, coming from a man whose body is so— I can't explain. I love your body. It's so wonderful and strong and—and unconquerable."

He laughed a little and challenged softly, "Conquer me."

There were no erotic games to be played this time, no painfully exciting torment. Luke pressed her back into the bedclothes, touching her breasts, her belly, her thighs, with abandon. He wanted her quickly, and that knowledge was enough to spark Grace's deepest desire. She teased him with feathery caresses, but they were not needed. This time they made love without preamble.

Grace drew Luke down to her, not allowing him to take command and lie beneath her as he had always preferred. She knew that he was cautious of his size. Luke had mastered every possible way of pleasing a woman without hurting her, but Grace had longed to feel him above her, taking her body with the swift abandon of passion as she reclined and reveled in the power of the act. He did it then, cradling her in his arms and sinking within her as smoothly and deeply as he could. For a long, exquisite moment, they lay locked together, breathing as one soul. Grace caressed his long, powerful back and whispered his name time and again.

Luke found her mouth with his. He kissed her there and moved to explore her throat. They began to move together, at some inner, magical signal, in a slow, savoring rhythm. It was good. It was delicious. It was full of emotion and relief. Together, they climbed the sensual heights, moving faster and more profoundly with each passing heartbeat.

For once Luke seemed to lose control. He thrust hard and fiercely, holding Grace so tightly that she clasped him in return and felt suddenly, wonderfully, a part of him, a part of his passion. She couldn't stop the cry that tore upward from inside her. Luke also groaned in relief, saying her name at the final intense moment of release.

Grace wrapped her weakened arms around his neck and pressed her cheek to his. "Oh, Luke. Please don't let me go away from you again. I've been such a—a pickle and I—"

Luke intervened by giving her a long, silencing kiss. He was firm, still full of excitement. With a deep, still love-hungry drive into her body, designed to bring her to complete surrender, he said, "Pickles are sour, and you're anything but that. So sweet, such a lady. So perfect."

Grace gave up with a happy sigh. "Can you stand such perfection, Luke? Really?"

"Yes," he said softly. "Come with me, Princess. Let's drive forever and make love in every hotel in every city in the country."

"And when we run out of cities?"

"We'll try another country."

Grace sighed. "That sounds like heaven. If we could only do it."

Luke braced himself on one elbow and met her eyes. His mouth had curved into a teasing smile, and the mischievous light was back in his eyes. "Why can't we?"

Smiling with him, Grace said, "I've kept you away from your business so long already . . ."

"A little longer won't matter," he said promptly. "I'm looking for a new place to open my garage anyway. We could check out every city between here and Seattle by the end of summer."

"Summer!"

"And then head east. We could—"

"Luke—"

"Hmm," he said thoughtfully, frowning a little. "We

might get into trouble in some of those supercivilized cities, though. We may have to get married here and avoid all the questions at check-in time."

Laughing, Grace said, "And it would certainly prevent you from bringing little blond surprises to sleep on the couch, wouldn't it?"

"That should never have happened," Luke explained in a rush. "I was being a Good Samaritan—honestly, Grace. I brought that girl downtown so she could get a bus to Chicago, but the bus didn't—"

"I don't want to hear it," Grace said firmly, tugging on the thick hair at the back of his neck. "Don't try to talk your way out of that one!"

He grinned slowly. "I love it when your nose twitches like that. What do you say, my love? Will you marry me?"

"Lucy didn't convince you that I'm unworthy? With terrible tales of my misguided youth?"

His eyes alight, Luke laughed again. "Boom-Boom Barrett's midnight swim in the college president's pool? With half the nearest fraternity—"

"I hope Lucy explained that *she* instigated all those—"

"No, no," Luke countered quickly, teasing her. "Don't try to talk your way out of this one, Princess! It's half your charm, you know. I can't imagine that anyone could be as ladylike and perfect as you pretend to be! Marry me, and we'll spend a lifetime figuring it out."

"Is that a proper marriage proposal, Laser?"

"Oh." He looked momentarily disconcerted. "Am I supposed to get down on one knee and— Oh, hell, I don't have to go talk to your father, do I? And your mother, too?"

"I'm not sure," Grace said lightly. "I suppose we'll have to consult a good etiquette book, won't we?"

*   *   *

Dear Ms. Barrett,
   I am planning my wedding, and I'm not sure how many attendants we should have. My fiancé has many

*friends who all want to wear tuxedos, but I was hoping
for a small, quiet affair with just family and our closest friends. What do you say?*

—Confused in Connecticut

Dear Confused,
  *Ms. Barrett is unavailable for comment. Write again
when she has returned from her honeymoon.*

QUESTIONNAIRE

1. How do you rate _____
                          (please print TITLE)
   ☐ excellent   ☐ good
   ☐ very good   ☐ fair   ☐ poor

2. How likely are you to purchase another book
   in this series?
   ☐ definitely would purchase
   ☐ probably would purchase
   ☐ probably would not purchase
   ☐ definitely would not purchase

3. How likely are you to purchase another book by
   this author?
   ☐ definitely would purchase
   ☐ probably would purchase
   ☐ probably would not purchase
   ☐ definitely would not purchase

4. How does this book compare to books in other
   contemporary romance lines?
   ☐ much better
   ☐ better
   ☐ about the same
   ☐ not as good
   ☐ definitely not as good

5. Why did you buy this book? (Check as many as apply)
   ☐ I have read other
       SECOND CHANCE AT LOVE romances
   ☐ friend's recommendation
   ☐ bookseller's recommendation
   ☐ art on the front cover
   ☐ description of the plot on the back cover
   ☐ book review I read
   ☐ other _____
       _____
       _____

(Continued...)

6. Please list your three favorite contemporary romance lines.

   _____
   _____

7. Please list your favorite authors of contemporary romance lines.

   _____
   _____
   _____
   _____
   _____
   _____

8. How many SECOND CHANCE AT LOVE romances have you read? _____

9. How many series romances like SECOND CHANCE AT LOVE do you <u>read</u> each month? _____

10. How many series romances like SECOND CHANCE AT LOVE do you <u>buy</u> each month? _____

11. Mind telling your age?
    ☐ under 18
    ☐ 18 to 30
    ☐ 31 to 45
    ☐ over 45

☐ Please check if you'd like to receive our <u>free</u> SECOND CHANCE AT LOVE Newsletter.

We hope you'll share your other ideas about romances with us on an additional sheet and attach it securely to this questionnaire.

· ·

Fill in your name and address below:
Name _____
Street Address _____
City _____ State _____ Zip _____

Please return this questionnaire to:
  SECOND CHANCE AT LOVE
  The Berkley Publishing Group
  200 Madison Avenue, New York, New York 10016